STONE ARCH BOOKS
a capstone imprint

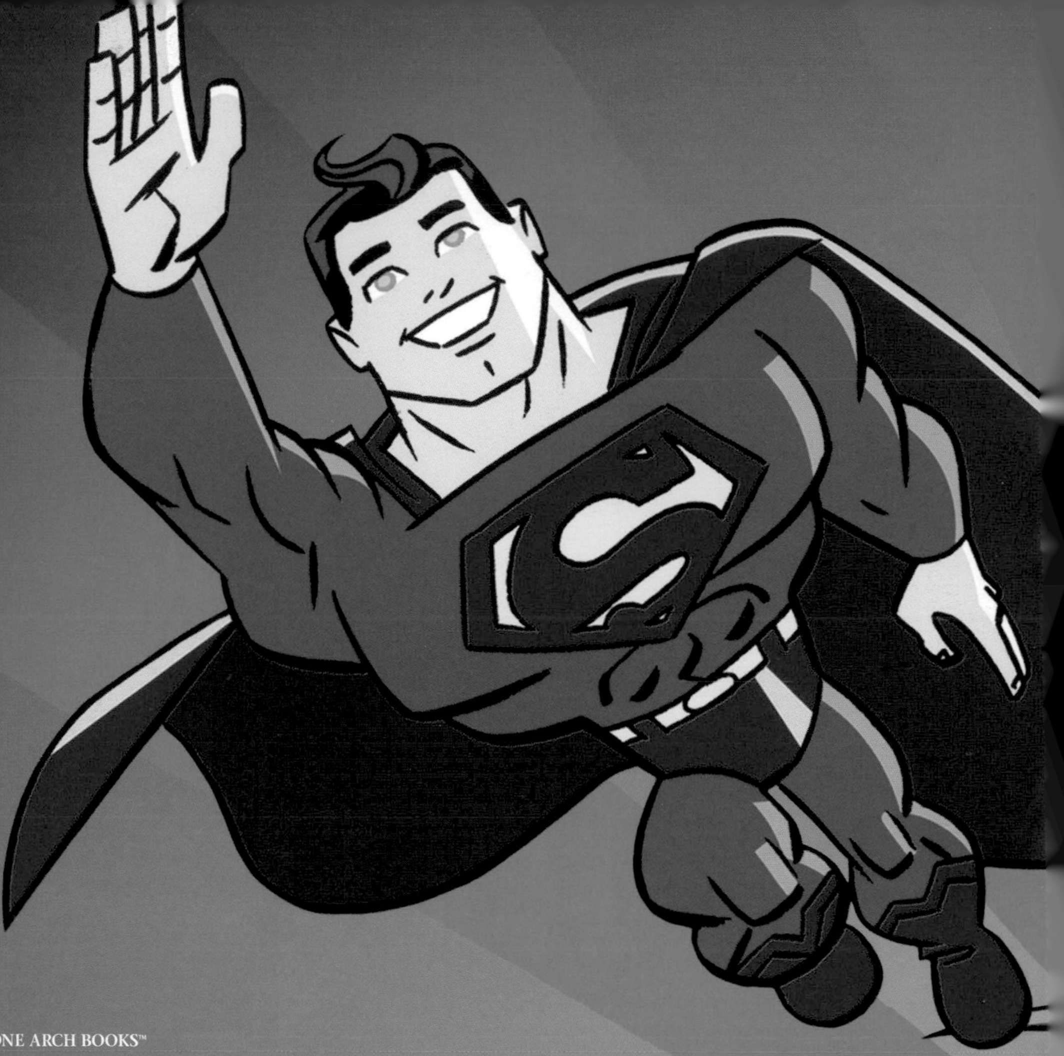

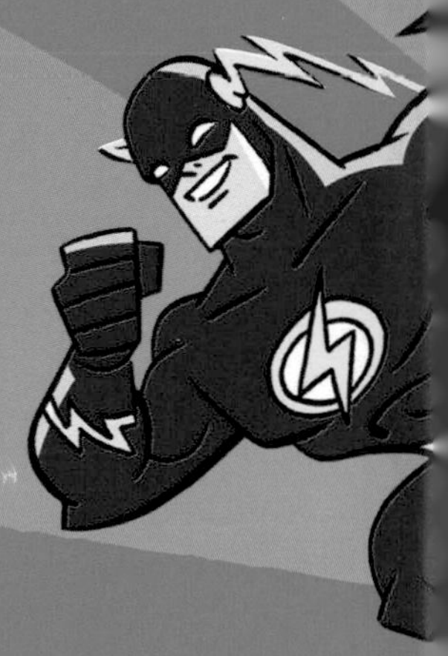

STONE ARCH BOOKS™
Published in 2012
A Capstone Imprint
1710 Roe Crest Drive
North Mankato, MN 56003
www.capstonepub.com

Originally published by DC Comics in
the U.S. in single magazine form as
DC Super Friends #3.


Cataloging-in-Publication Data is available at the
Library of Congress website:
ISBN: 978-1-4342-4543-4 (library binding)

Summary: The World's Greatest Super Heroes are here to save the day - and be your friends, too! Follow along as the Super Friends spiral out of control! Will they discover who's in charge of them before they have to retire for good?

*STONE ARCH BOOKS*
Ashley C. Andersen Zantop *Publisher*
Michael Dahl *Editorial Director*
Donald Lemke & Julie Gassman *Editors*
Heather Kindseth *Creative Director*
Brann Garvey *Designer*
Kathy McColley *Production Specialist*

*DC COMICS*
Rachel Gluckstern *Original U.S. Editor*

Printed and bound in the USA.
009770R

DC Comics
1700 Broadway, New York, NY 10019
A Warner Bros. Entertainment Company

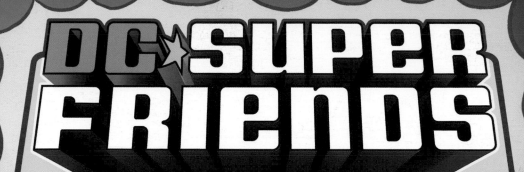

# DC SUPER FRIENDS

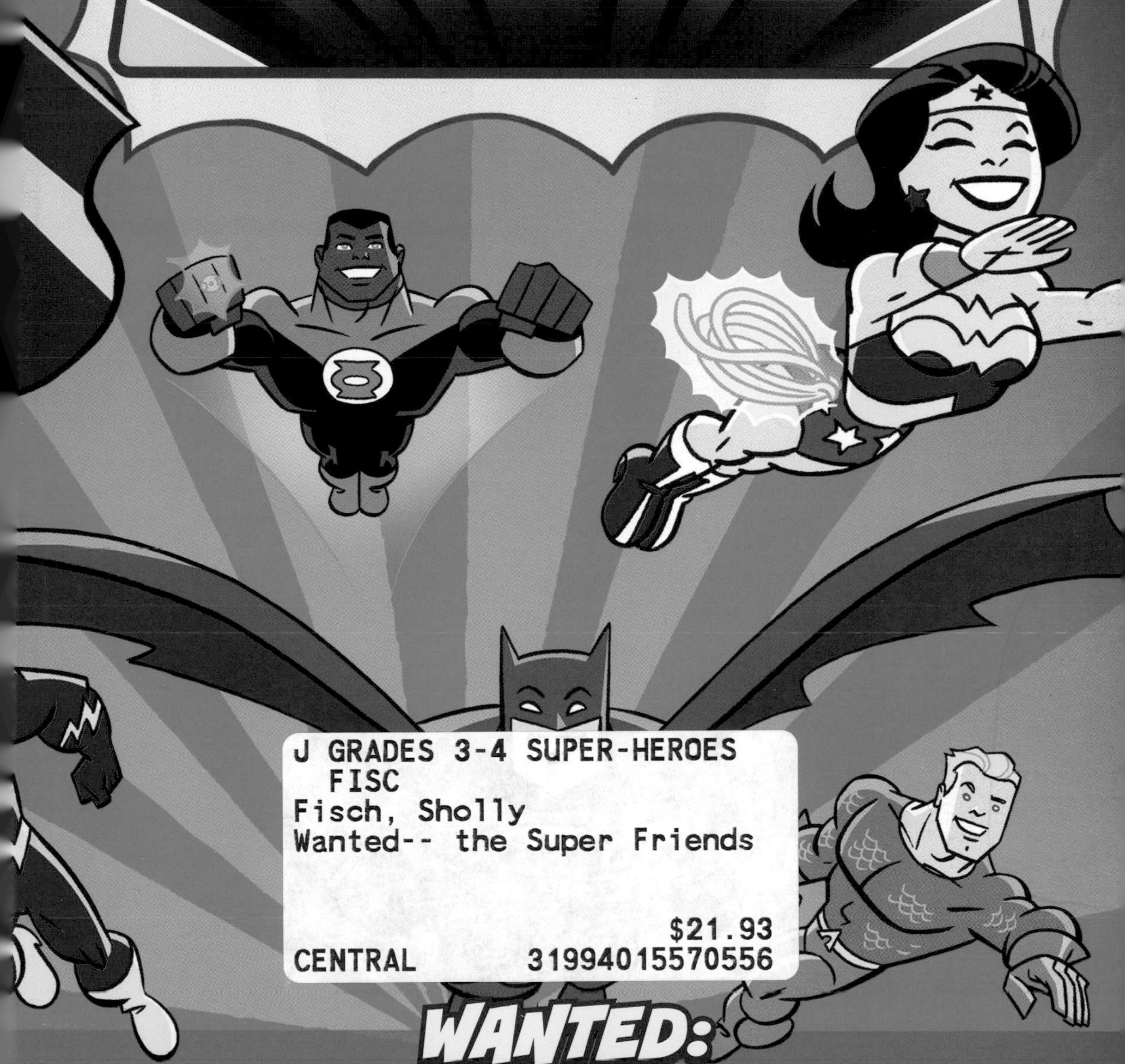



# WANTED: THE SUPER FRIENDS

Sholly Fisch ............................writer
Stewart McKenny ..................artist
Phil Moy..................................inker
Heroic Age .......................... colorist
Rob Clark, Jr. .....................letterer
J. Bone .........................cover artist

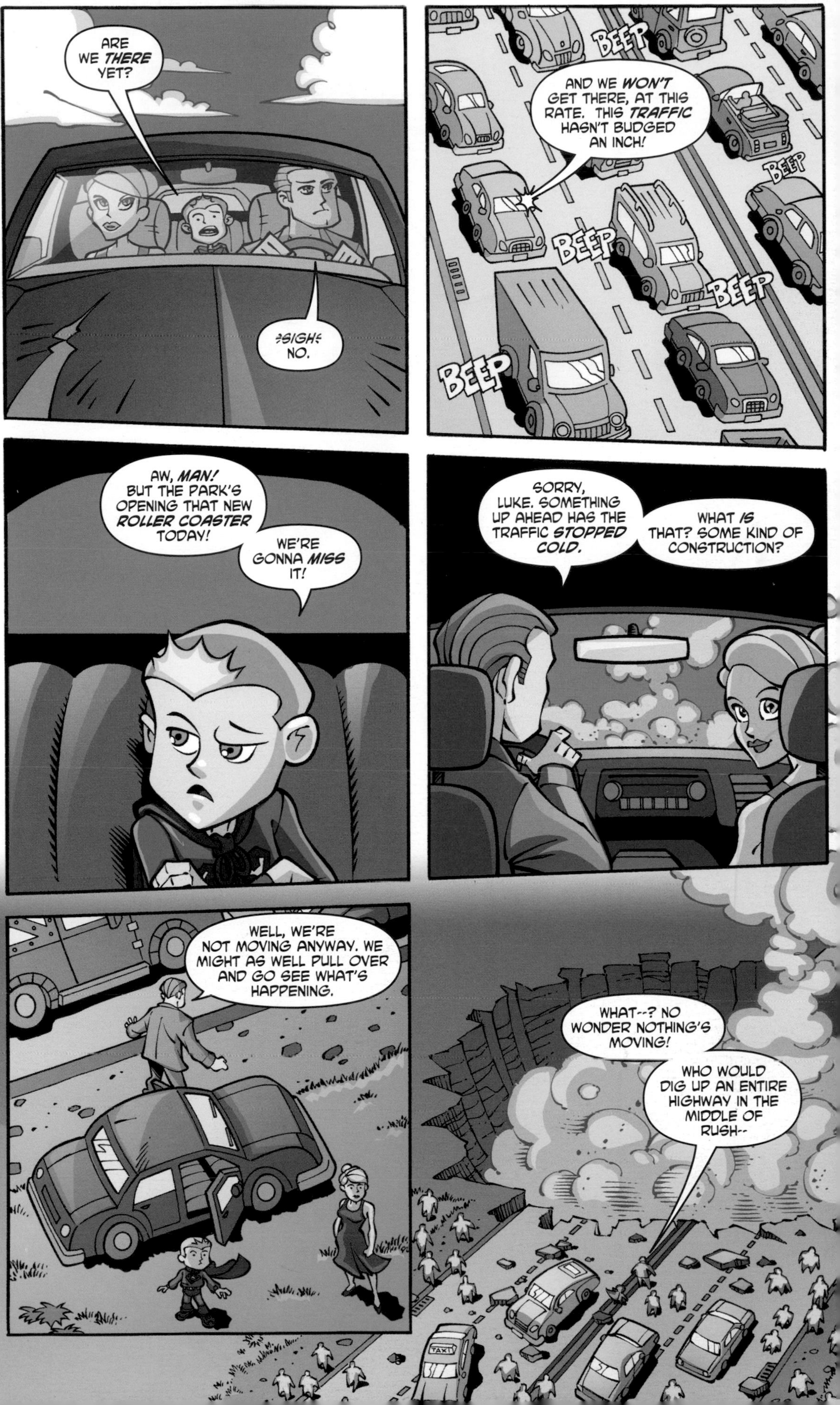
ARE WE *THERE* YET?
*SIGH* NO.
BEEP
AND WE *WON'T* GET THERE, AT THIS RATE. THIS *TRAFFIC* HASN'T BUDGED AN INCH!
BEEP
BEEP
BEEP
BEEP
AW, *MAN!* BUT THE PARK'S OPENING THAT NEW *ROLLER COASTER* TODAY!
WE'RE GONNA *MISS* IT!
SORRY, LUKE. SOMETHING UP AHEAD HAS THE TRAFFIC *STOPPED COLD.*
WHAT *IS* THAT? SOME KIND OF CONSTRUCTION?
WELL, WE'RE NOT MOVING ANYWAY. WE MIGHT AS WELL PULL OVER AND GO SEE WHAT'S HAPPENING.
WHAT--? NO WONDER NOTHING'S MOVING!
WHO WOULD DIG UP AN ENTIRE HIGHWAY IN THE MIDDLE OF RUSH--
TAXI

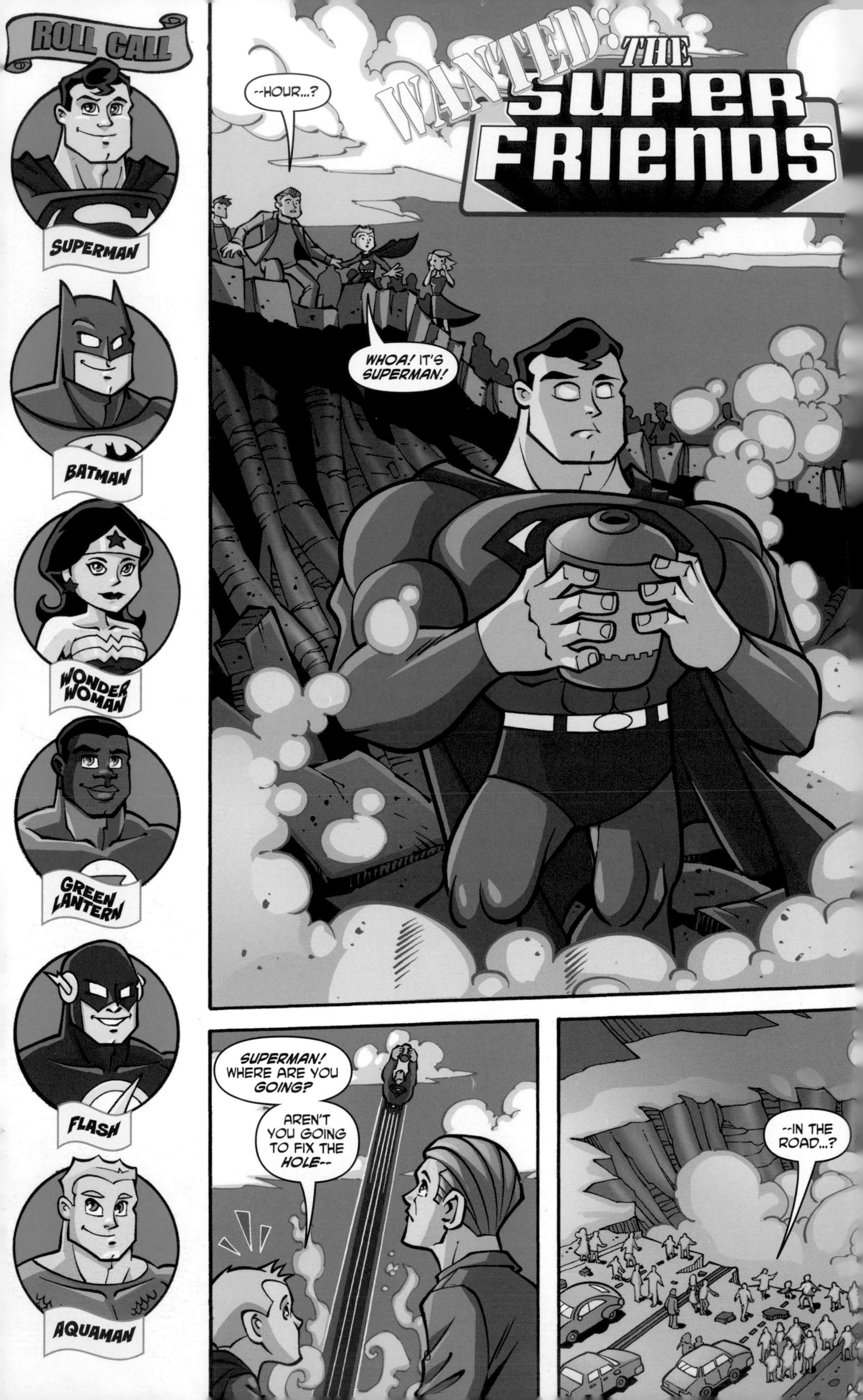
ROLL CALL
SUPERMAN
BATMAN
WONDER WOMAN
GREEN LANTERN
FLASH
AQUAMAN
WANTED: THE SUPER FRIENDS
--HOUR...?
WHOA! IT'S SUPERMAN!
SUPERMAN! WHERE ARE YOU GOING?
AREN'T YOU GOING TO FIX THE HOLE--
--IN THE ROAD...?

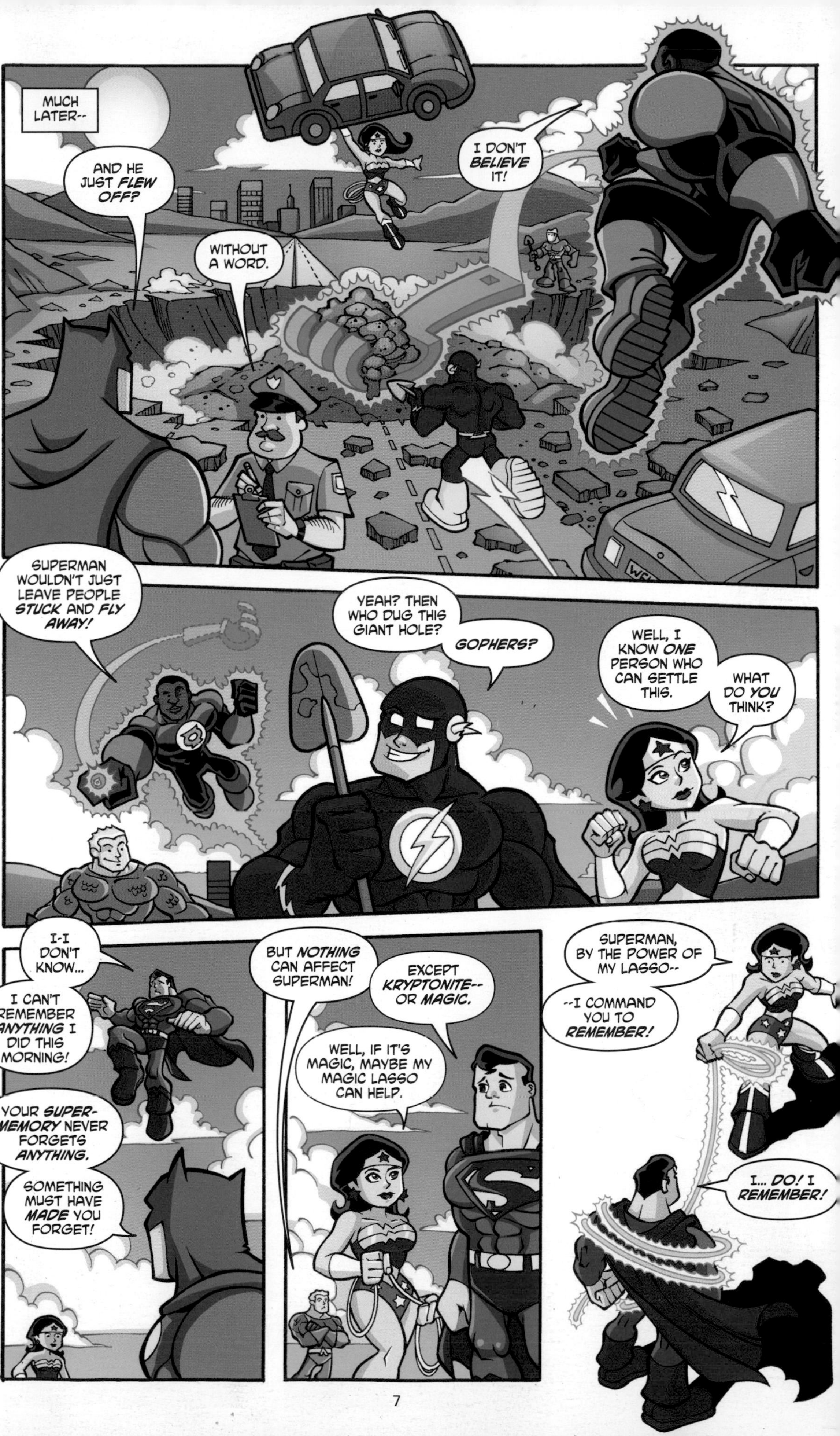
MUCH LATER--
AND HE JUST FLEW OFF?
WITHOUT A WORD.
I DON'T BELIEVE IT!
SUPERMAN WOULDN'T JUST LEAVE PEOPLE STUCK AND FLY AWAY!
YEAH? THEN WHO DUG THIS GIANT HOLE?
GOPHERS?
WELL, I KNOW ONE PERSON WHO CAN SETTLE THIS.
WHAT DO YOU THINK?
I-I DON'T KNOW...
I CAN'T REMEMBER ANYTHING I DID THIS MORNING!
YOUR SUPER-MEMORY NEVER FORGETS ANYTHING.
SOMETHING MUST HAVE MADE YOU FORGET!
BUT NOTHING CAN AFFECT SUPERMAN!
EXCEPT KRYPTONITE-- OR MAGIC.
WELL, IF IT'S MAGIC, MAYBE MY MAGIC LASSO CAN HELP.
SUPERMAN, BY THE POWER OF MY LASSO--
--I COMMAND YOU TO REMEMBER!
I... DO! I REMEMBER!

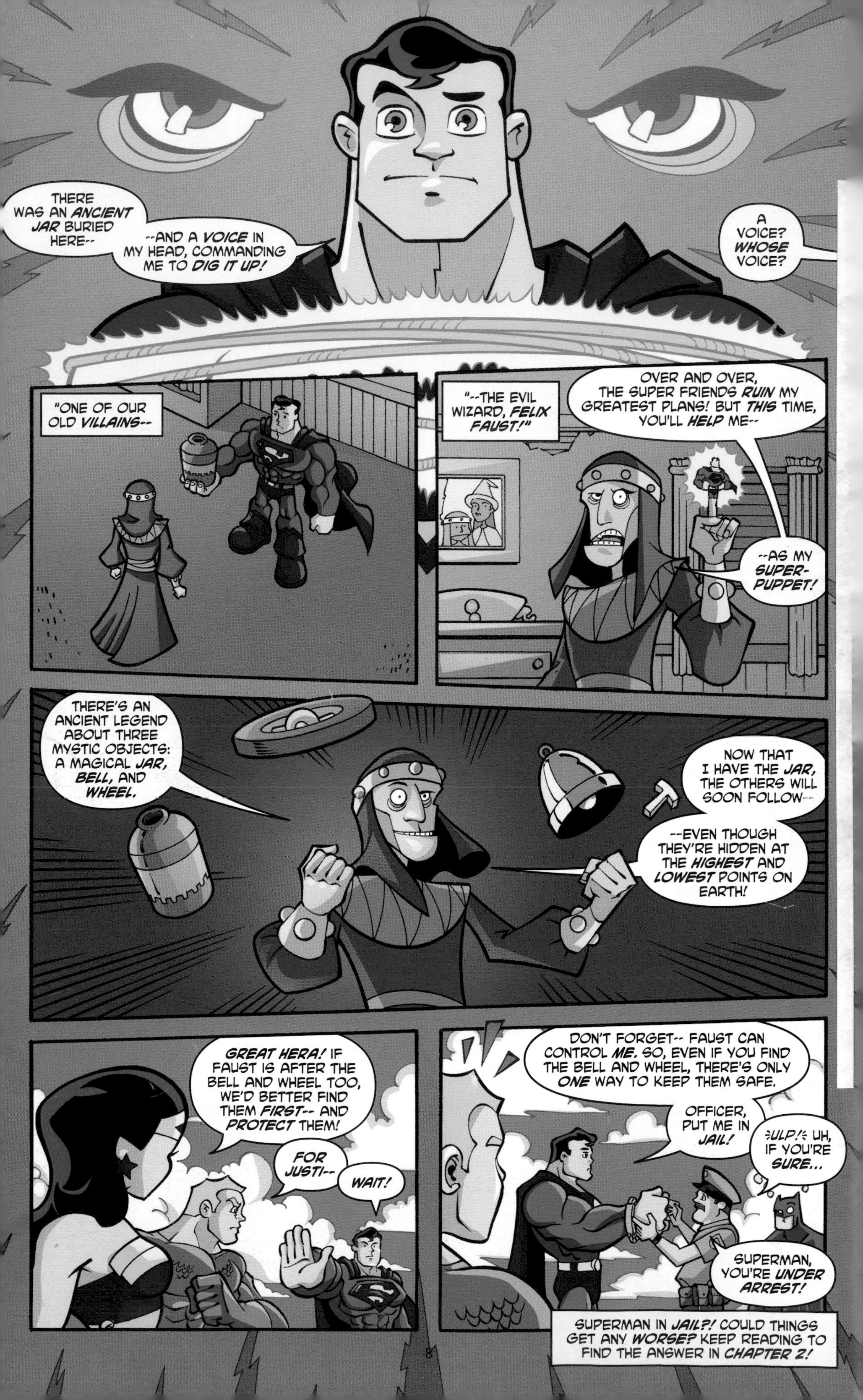

THERE WAS AN ANCIENT JAR BURIED HERE--
--AND A VOICE IN MY HEAD, COMMANDING ME TO DIG IT UP!
A VOICE? WHOSE VOICE?
"ONE OF OUR OLD VILLAINS--
"--THE EVIL WIZARD, FELIX FAUST!"
OVER AND OVER, THE SUPER FRIENDS RUIN MY GREATEST PLANS! BUT THIS TIME, YOU'LL HELP ME--
--AS MY SUPER-PUPPET!
THERE'S AN ANCIENT LEGEND ABOUT THREE MYSTIC OBJECTS: A MAGICAL JAR, BELL, AND WHEEL.
NOW THAT I HAVE THE JAR, THE OTHERS WILL SOON FOLLOW--
--EVEN THOUGH THEY'RE HIDDEN AT THE HIGHEST AND LOWEST POINTS ON EARTH!
GREAT HERA! IF FAUST IS AFTER THE BELL AND WHEEL TOO, WE'D BETTER FIND THEM FIRST-- AND PROTECT THEM!
FOR JUSTI--
WAIT!
DON'T FORGET-- FAUST CAN CONTROL ME. SO, EVEN IF YOU FIND THE BELL AND WHEEL, THERE'S ONLY ONE WAY TO KEEP THEM SAFE.
OFFICER, PUT ME IN JAIL!
ULP! UH, IF YOU'RE SURE...
SUPERMAN, YOU'RE UNDER ARREST!
SUPERMAN IN JAIL?! COULD THINGS GET ANY WORSE? KEEP READING TO FIND THE ANSWER IN CHAPTER 2!

# WANTED: THE SUPER FRIENDS PART 2

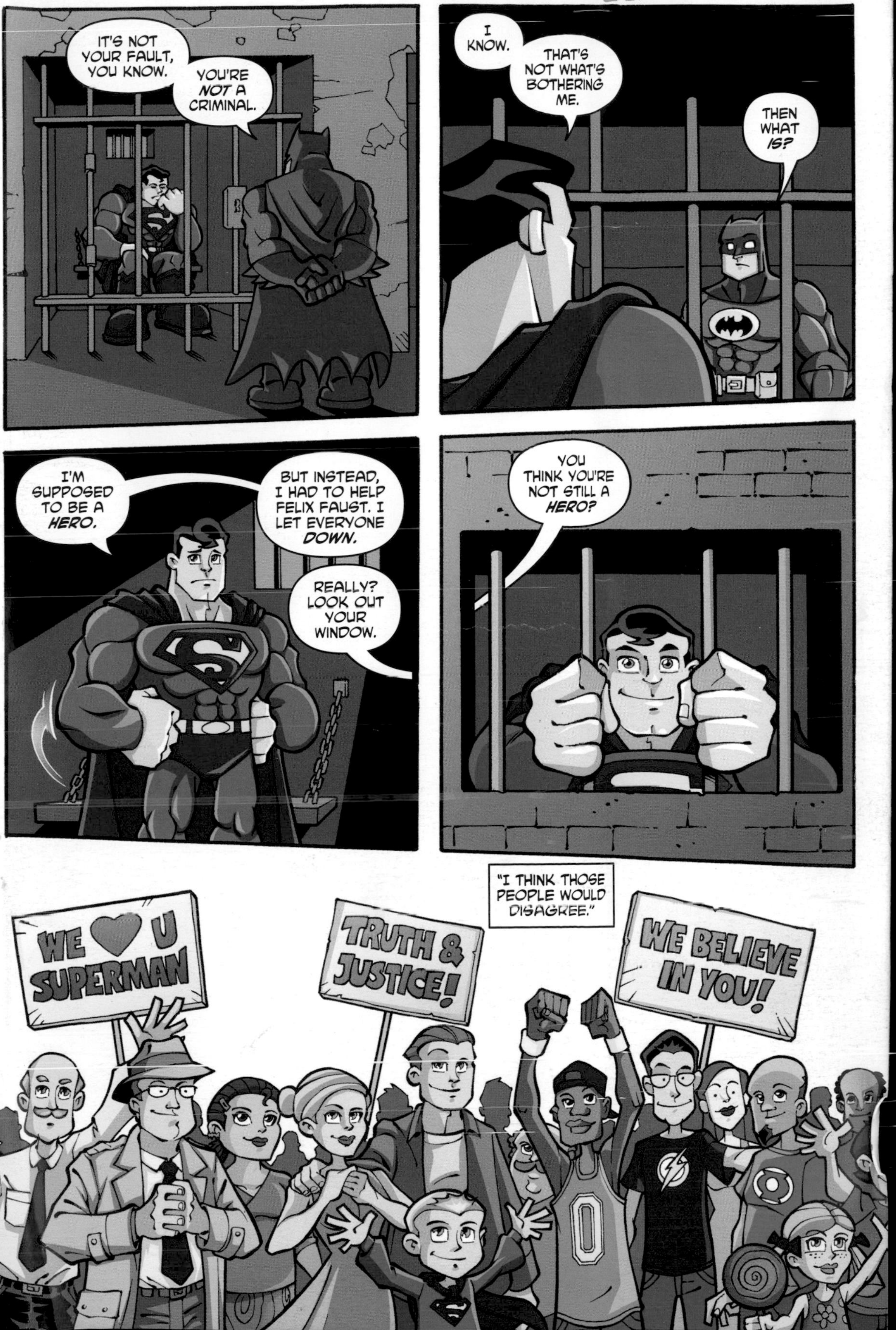

IT'S NOT YOUR FAULT, YOU KNOW.
YOU'RE *NOT* A CRIMINAL.
I KNOW.
THAT'S NOT WHAT'S BOTHERING ME.
THEN WHAT *IS?*
I'M SUPPOSED TO BE A *HERO.*
BUT INSTEAD, I HAD TO HELP FELIX FAUST. I LET EVERYONE *DOWN.*
REALLY? LOOK OUT YOUR WINDOW.
YOU THINK YOU'RE NOT STILL A *HERO?*
"I THINK THOSE PEOPLE WOULD DISAGREE."
WE ♥ U SUPERMAN
TRUTH & JUSTICE!
WE BELIEVE IN YOU!

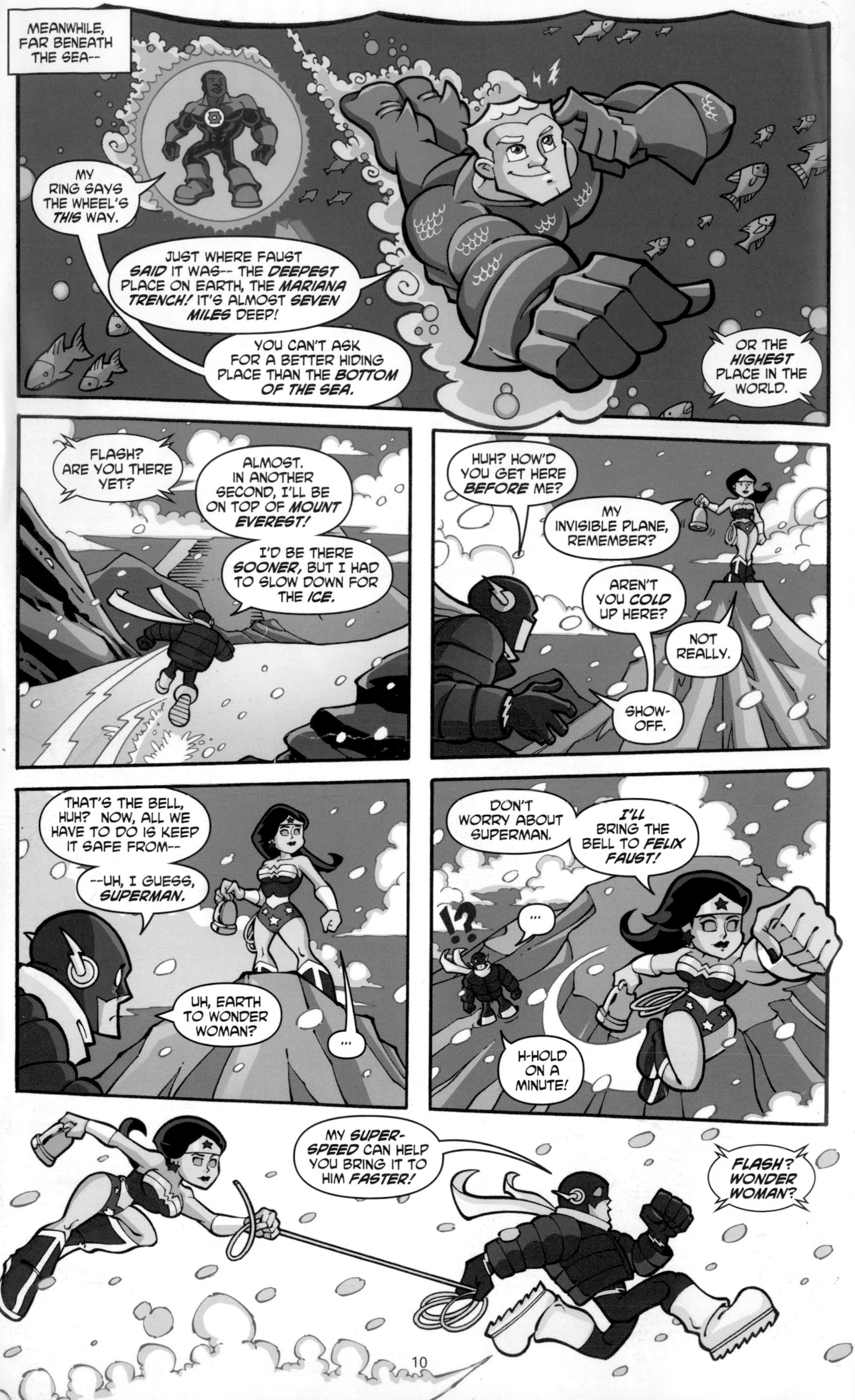

MEANWHILE, FAR BENEATH THE SEA--
MY RING SAYS THE WHEEL'S *THIS* WAY.
JUST WHERE FAUST *SAID* IT WAS-- THE *DEEPEST* PLACE ON EARTH, THE *MARIANA TRENCH!* IT'S ALMOST *SEVEN MILES* DEEP!
YOU CAN'T ASK FOR A BETTER HIDING PLACE THAN THE *BOTTOM OF THE SEA.*
OR THE *HIGHEST* PLACE IN THE WORLD.
FLASH? ARE YOU THERE YET?
ALMOST. IN ANOTHER SECOND, I'LL BE ON TOP OF *MOUNT EVEREST!*
I'D BE THERE *SOONER,* BUT I HAD TO SLOW DOWN FOR THE *ICE.*
HUH? HOW'D YOU GET HERE *BEFORE* ME?
MY INVISIBLE PLANE, REMEMBER?
AREN'T YOU *COLD* UP HERE?
NOT REALLY.
SHOW-OFF.
THAT'S THE BELL, HUH? NOW, ALL WE HAVE TO DO IS KEEP IT SAFE FROM--
--UH, I GUESS, *SUPERMAN.*
UH, EARTH TO WONDER WOMAN?
...
DON'T WORRY ABOUT SUPERMAN.
*I'LL* BRING THE BELL TO *FELIX FAUST!*
...
!?
H-HOLD ON A MINUTE!
MY *SUPER-SPEED* CAN HELP YOU BRING IT TO HIM *FASTER!*
*FLASH? WONDER WOMAN?*

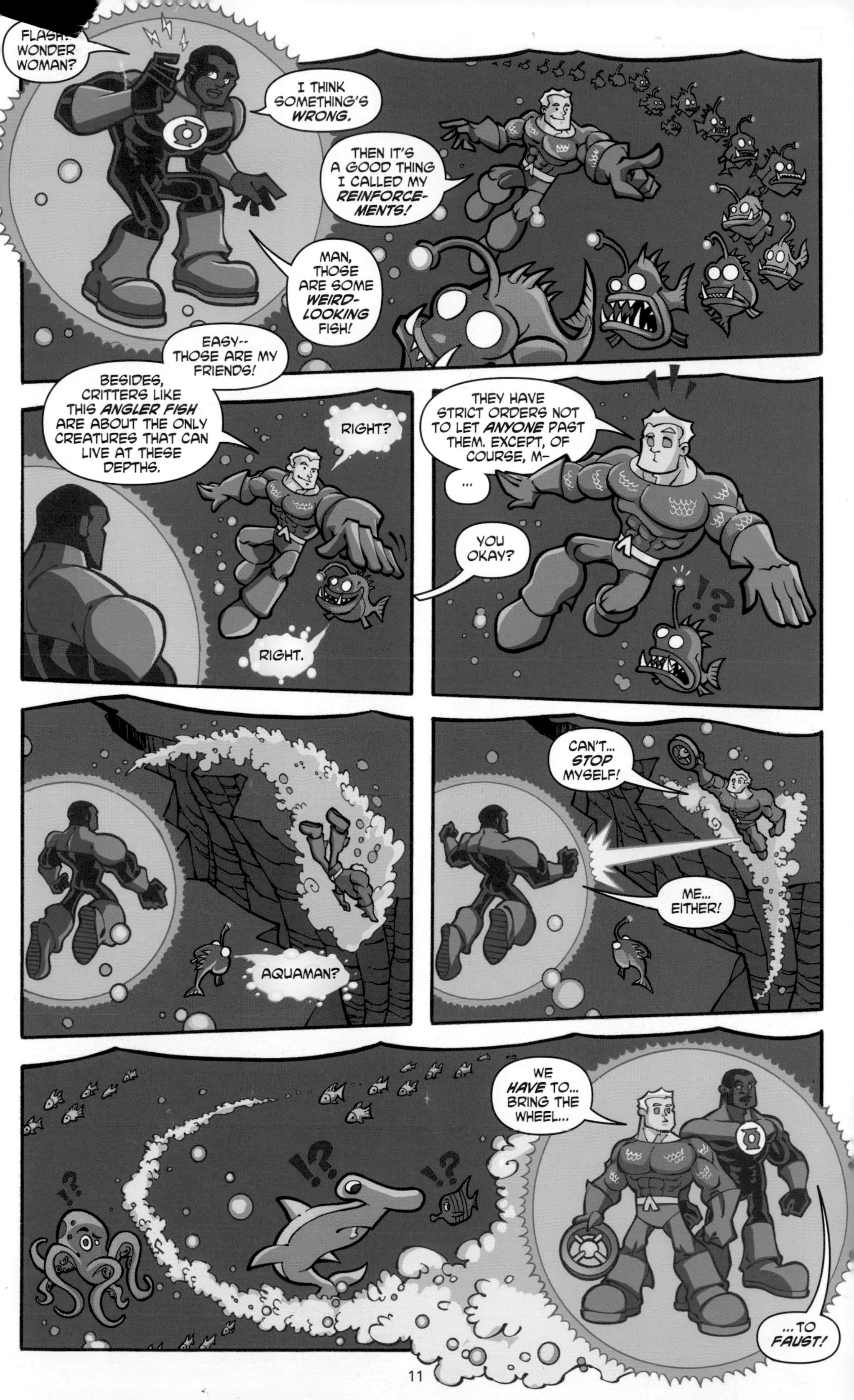
FLASH? WONDER WOMAN?
I THINK SOMETHING'S WRONG.
THEN IT'S A GOOD THING I CALLED MY REINFORCE-MENTS!
MAN, THOSE ARE SOME WEIRD-LOOKING FISH!
EASY-- THOSE ARE MY FRIENDS!
BESIDES, CRITTERS LIKE THIS ANGLER FISH ARE ABOUT THE ONLY CREATURES THAT CAN LIVE AT THESE DEPTHS.
RIGHT?
RIGHT.
THEY HAVE STRICT ORDERS NOT TO LET ANYONE PAST THEM. EXCEPT, OF COURSE, M-
...
YOU OKAY?
!?
AQUAMAN?
CAN'T... STOP MYSELF!
ME... EITHER!
!?
!?
!?
WE HAVE TO... BRING THE WHEEL...
...TO FAUST!

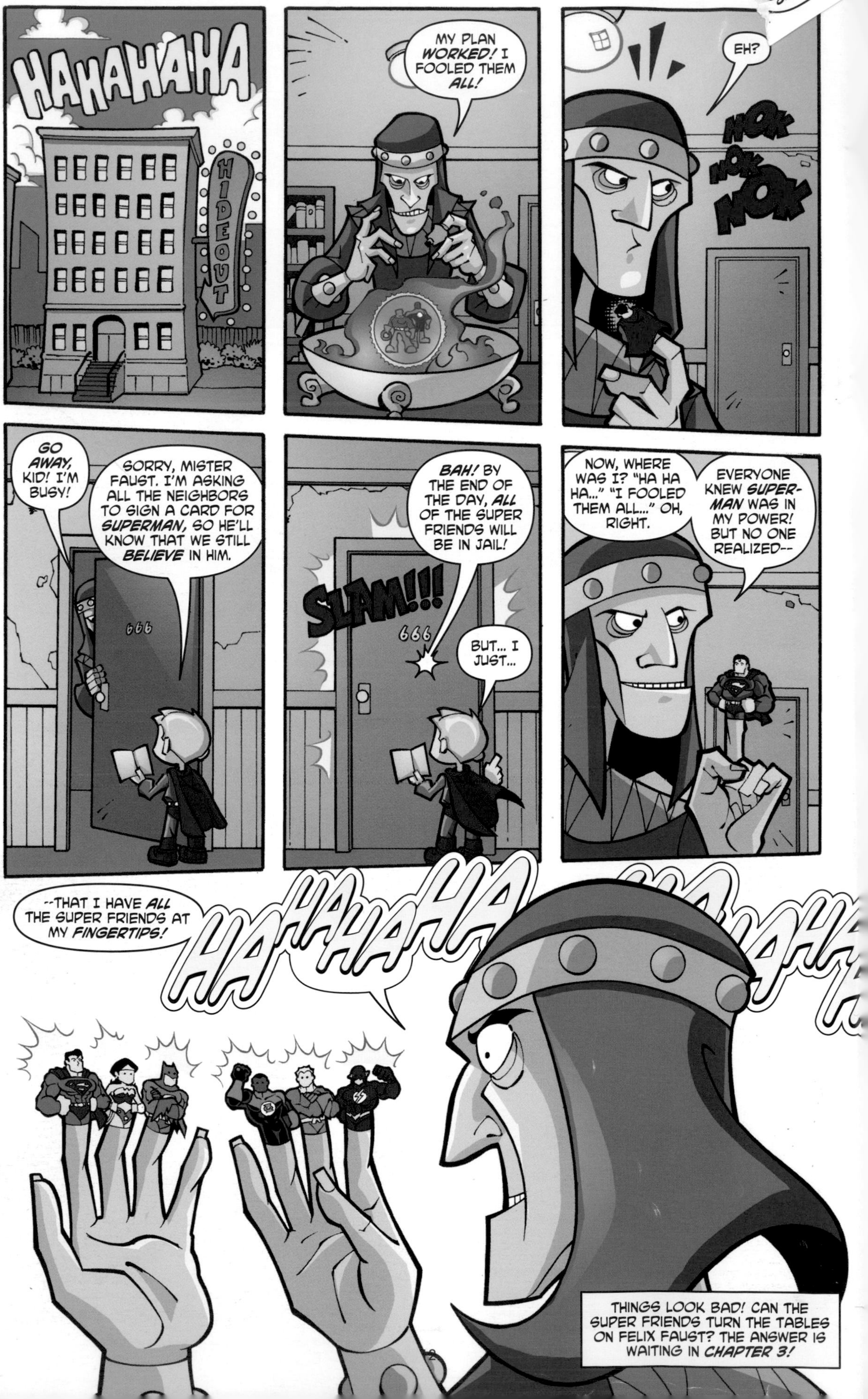
HAHAHAHA
HIDEOUT
MY PLAN WORKED! I FOOLED THEM ALL!
EH?
NOK NOK NOK
GO AWAY, KID! I'M BUSY!
SORRY, MISTER FAUST. I'M ASKING ALL THE NEIGHBORS TO SIGN A CARD FOR SUPERMAN, SO HE'LL KNOW THAT WE STILL BELIEVE IN HIM.
666
BAH! BY THE END OF THE DAY, ALL OF THE SUPER FRIENDS WILL BE IN JAIL!
SLAM!!!
666
BUT... I JUST...
NOW, WHERE WAS I? "HA HA HA..." "I FOOLED THEM ALL..." OH, RIGHT.
EVERYONE KNEW SUPERMAN WAS IN MY POWER! BUT NO ONE REALIZED--
--THAT I HAVE ALL THE SUPER FRIENDS AT MY FINGERTIPS!
HAHAHAHA
THINGS LOOK BAD! CAN THE SUPER FRIENDS TURN THE TABLES ON FELIX FAUST? THE ANSWER IS WAITING IN CHAPTER 3!

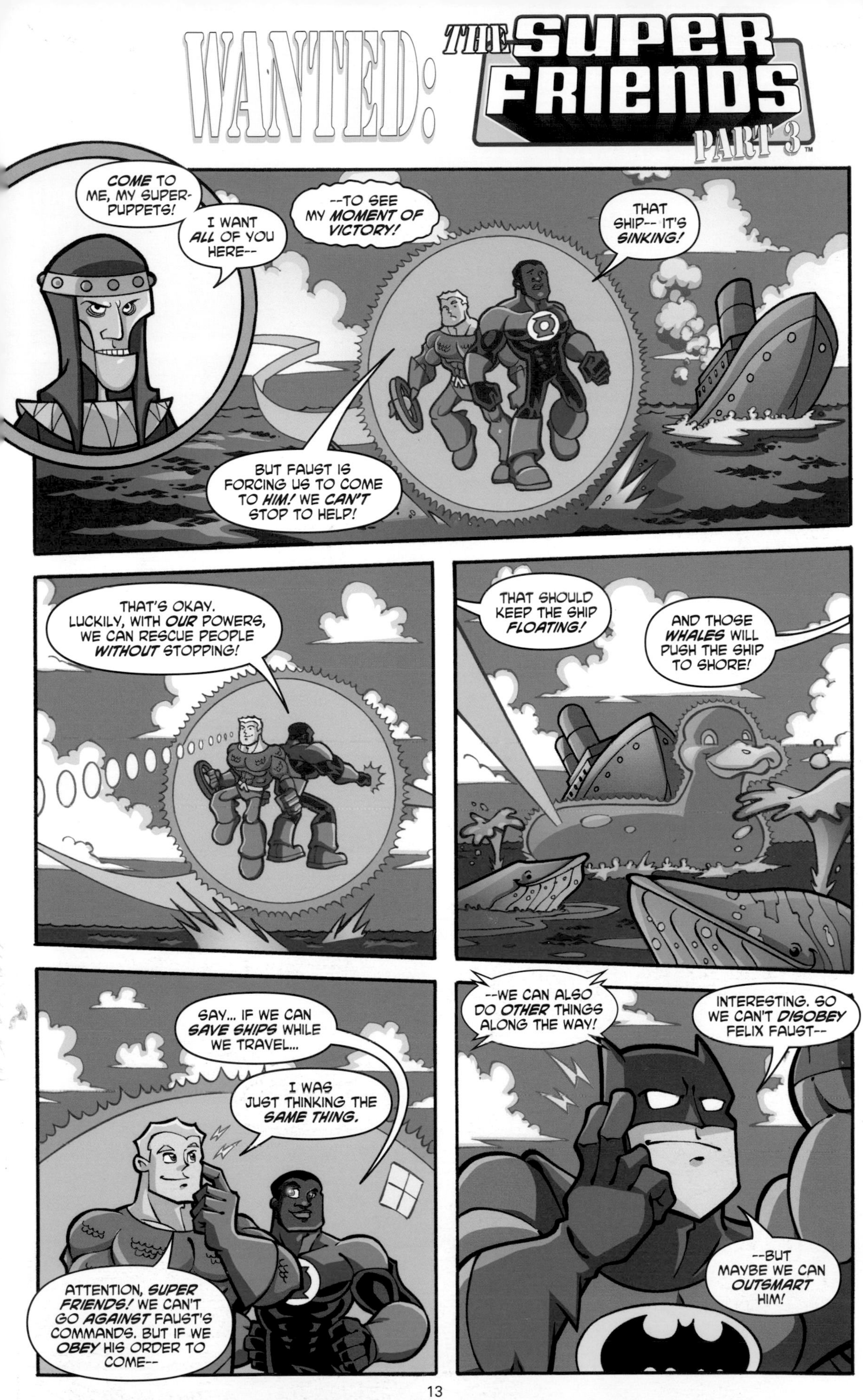
WANTED: THE SUPER FRIENDS PART 3
COME TO ME, MY SUPER-PUPPETS!
I WANT ALL OF YOU HERE--
--TO SEE MY MOMENT OF VICTORY!
THAT SHIP-- IT'S SINKING!
BUT FAUST IS FORCING US TO COME TO HIM! WE CAN'T STOP TO HELP!
THAT'S OKAY. LUCKILY, WITH OUR POWERS, WE CAN RESCUE PEOPLE WITHOUT STOPPING!
THAT SHOULD KEEP THE SHIP FLOATING!
AND THOSE WHALES WILL PUSH THE SHIP TO SHORE!
SAY... IF WE CAN SAVE SHIPS WHILE WE TRAVEL...
I WAS JUST THINKING THE SAME THING.
ATTENTION, SUPER FRIENDS! WE CAN'T GO AGAINST FAUST'S COMMANDS. BUT IF WE OBEY HIS ORDER TO COME--
--WE CAN ALSO DO OTHER THINGS ALONG THE WAY!
INTERESTING. SO WE CAN'T DISOBEY FELIX FAUST--
--BUT MAYBE WE CAN OUTSMART HIM!

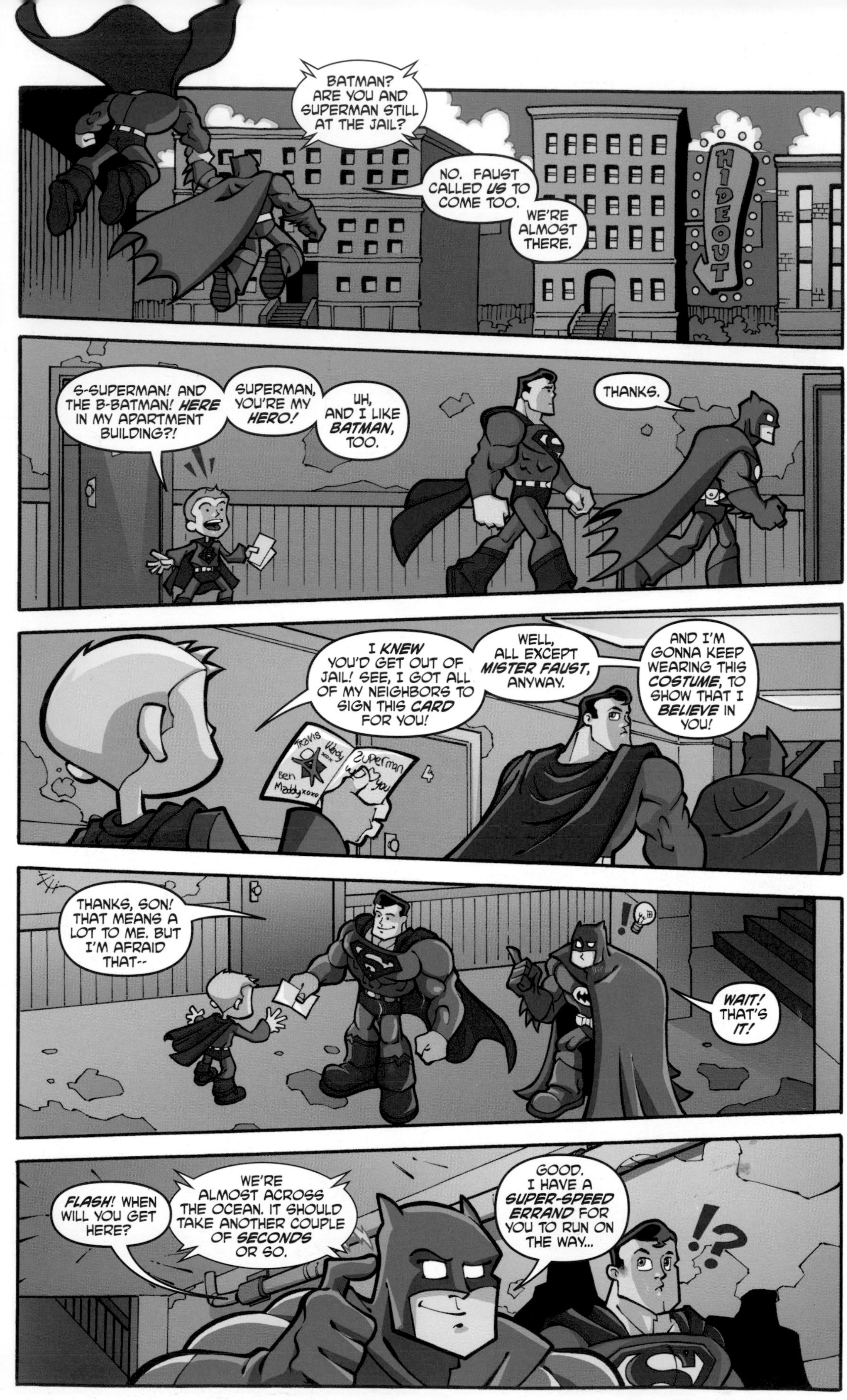
BATMAN? ARE YOU AND SUPERMAN STILL AT THE JAIL?
NO. FAUST CALLED US TO COME TOO.
WE'RE ALMOST THERE.
HIDEOUT
S-SUPERMAN! AND THE B-BATMAN! HERE IN MY APARTMENT BUILDING?!
SUPERMAN, YOU'RE MY HERO!
UH, AND I LIKE BATMAN, TOO.
THANKS.
I KNEW YOU'D GET OUT OF JAIL! SEE, I GOT ALL OF MY NEIGHBORS TO SIGN THIS CARD FOR YOU!
WELL, ALL EXCEPT MISTER FAUST, ANYWAY.
AND I'M GONNA KEEP WEARING THIS COSTUME, TO SHOW THAT I BELIEVE IN YOU!
THANKS, SON! THAT MEANS A LOT TO ME. BUT I'M AFRAID THAT--
WAIT! THAT'S IT!
FLASH! WHEN WILL YOU GET HERE?
WE'RE ALMOST ACROSS THE OCEAN. IT SHOULD TAKE ANOTHER COUPLE OF SECONDS OR SO.
GOOD. I HAVE A SUPER-SPEED ERRAND FOR YOU TO RUN ON THE WAY...

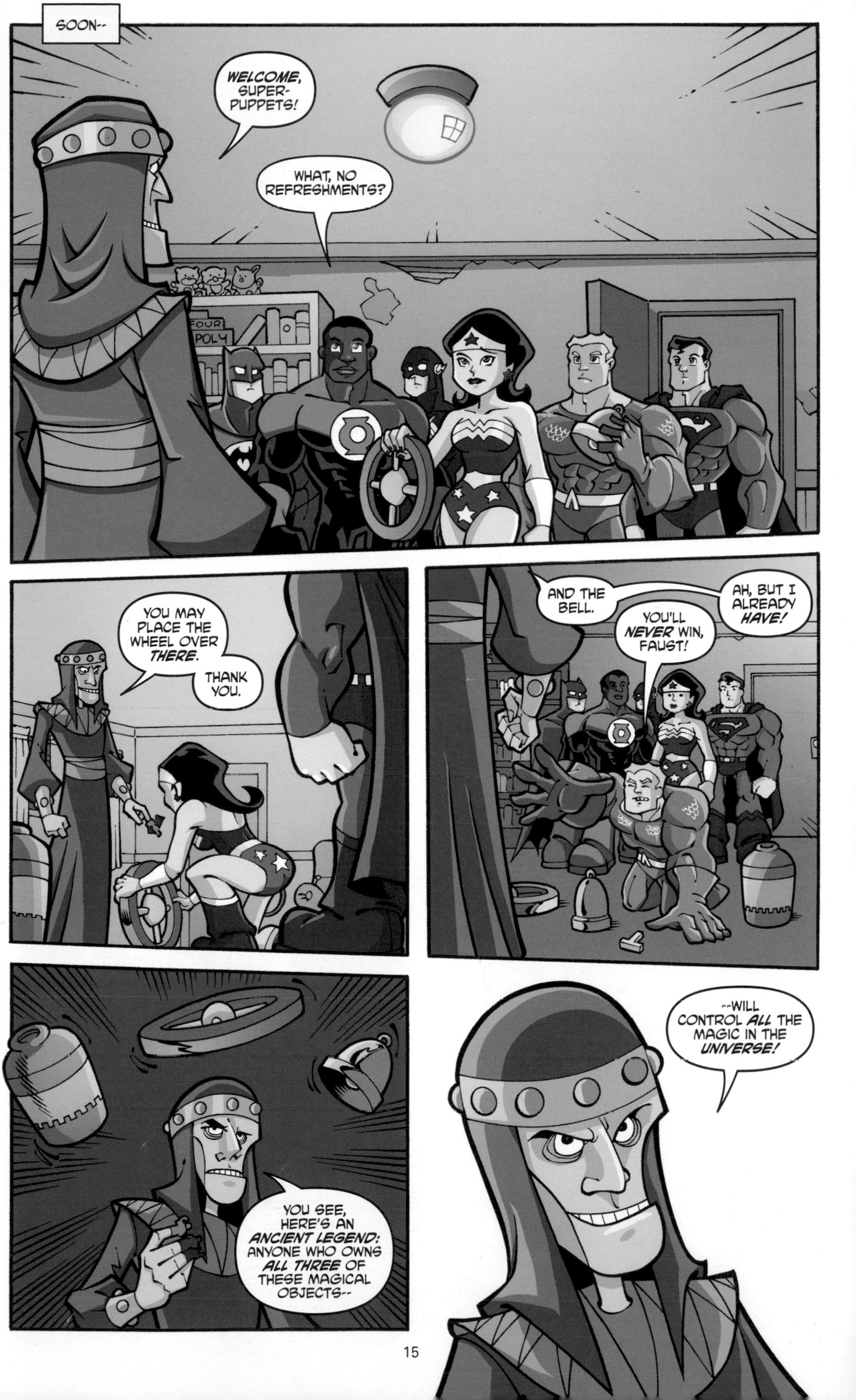
SOON--
WELCOME, SUPER-PUPPETS!
WHAT, NO REFRESHMENTS?
FOUR
POLY
YOU MAY PLACE THE WHEEL OVER THERE.
THANK YOU.
AND THE BELL.
YOU'LL NEVER WIN, FAUST!
AH, BUT I ALREADY HAVE!
YOU SEE, HERE'S AN ANCIENT LEGEND: ANYONE WHO OWNS ALL THREE OF THESE MAGICAL OBJECTS--
--WILL CONTROL ALL THE MAGIC IN THE UNIVERSE!

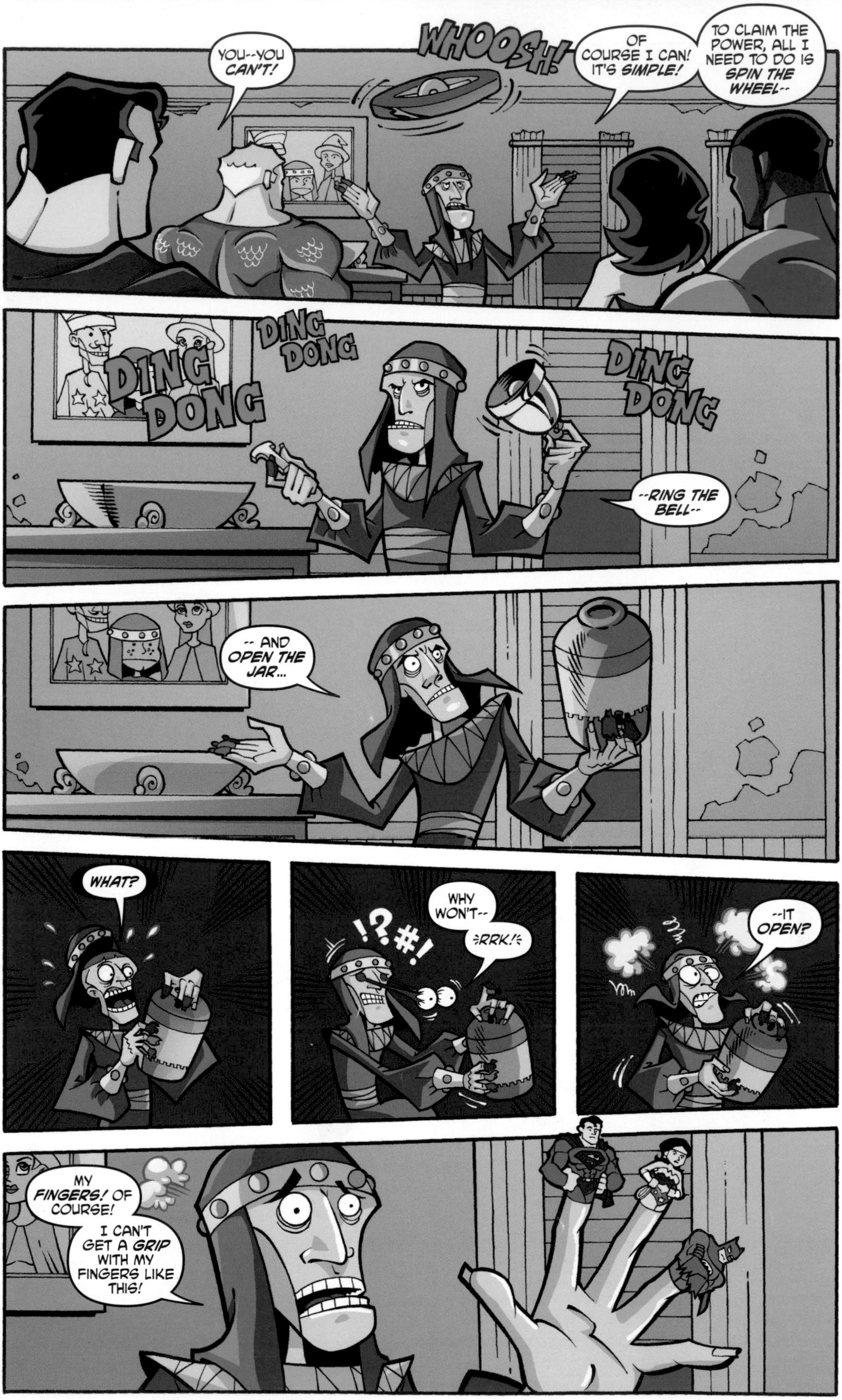
YOU--YOU CAN'T!
WHOOSH!
OF COURSE I CAN! IT'S SIMPLE!
TO CLAIM THE POWER, ALL I NEED TO DO IS SPIN THE WHEEL--
DING DONG
DING DONG
DING DONG
--RING THE BELL--
-- AND OPEN THE JAR...
WHAT?
WHY WON'T--
RRK!
!?#!
--IT OPEN?
MY FINGERS! OF COURSE!
I CAN'T GET A GRIP WITH MY FINGERS LIKE THIS!

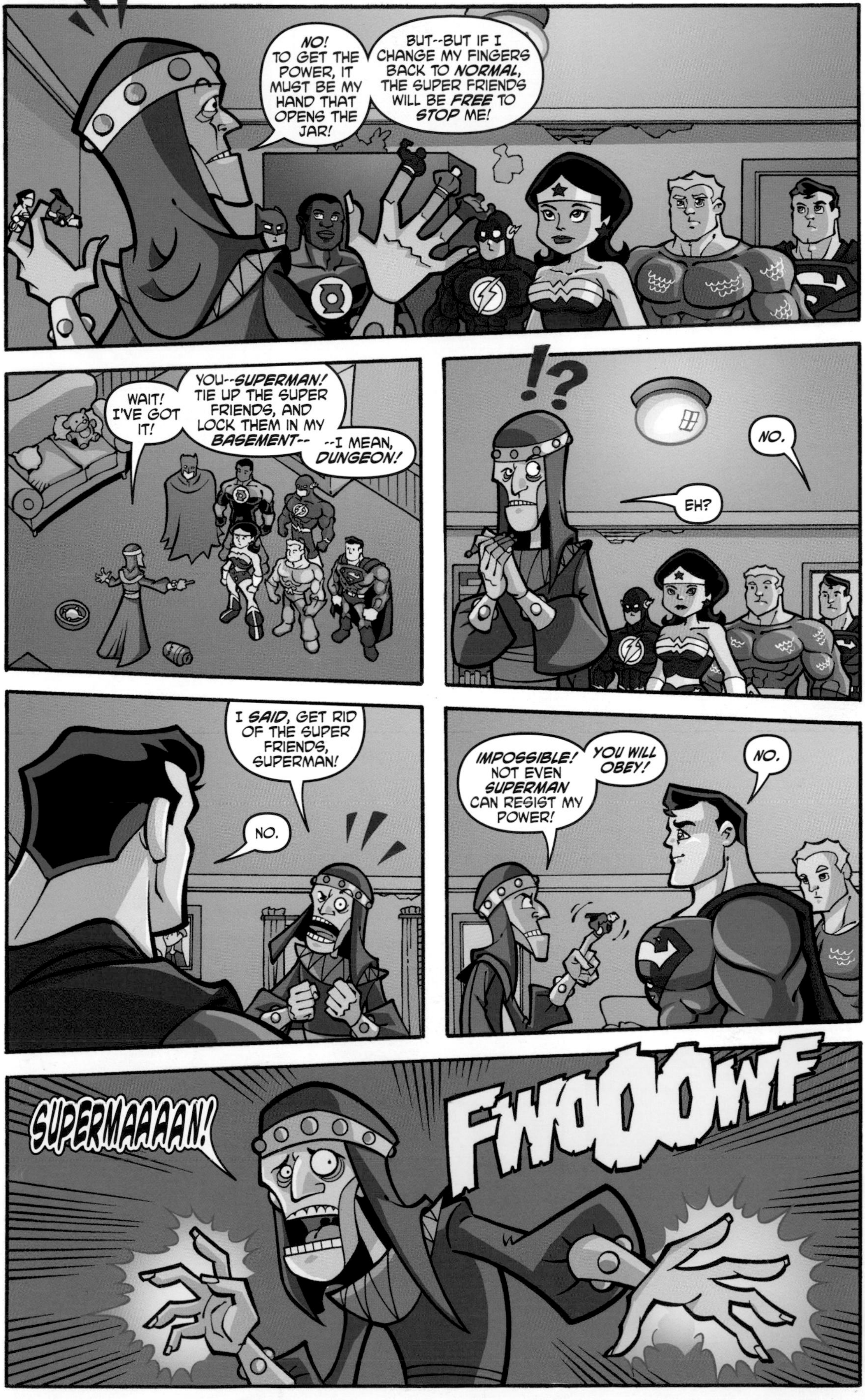
NO! TO GET THE POWER, IT MUST BE MY HAND THAT OPENS THE JAR!
BUT--BUT IF I CHANGE MY FINGERS BACK TO NORMAL, THE SUPER FRIENDS WILL BE FREE TO STOP ME!
WAIT! I'VE GOT IT!
YOU--SUPERMAN! TIE UP THE SUPER FRIENDS, AND LOCK THEM IN MY BASEMENT--
--I MEAN, DUNGEON!
!?
NO.
EH?
I SAID, GET RID OF THE SUPER FRIENDS, SUPERMAN!
NO.
IMPOSSIBLE! NOT EVEN SUPERMAN CAN RESIST MY POWER!
YOU WILL OBEY!
NO.
SUPERMAAAAN!
FWOOOWF

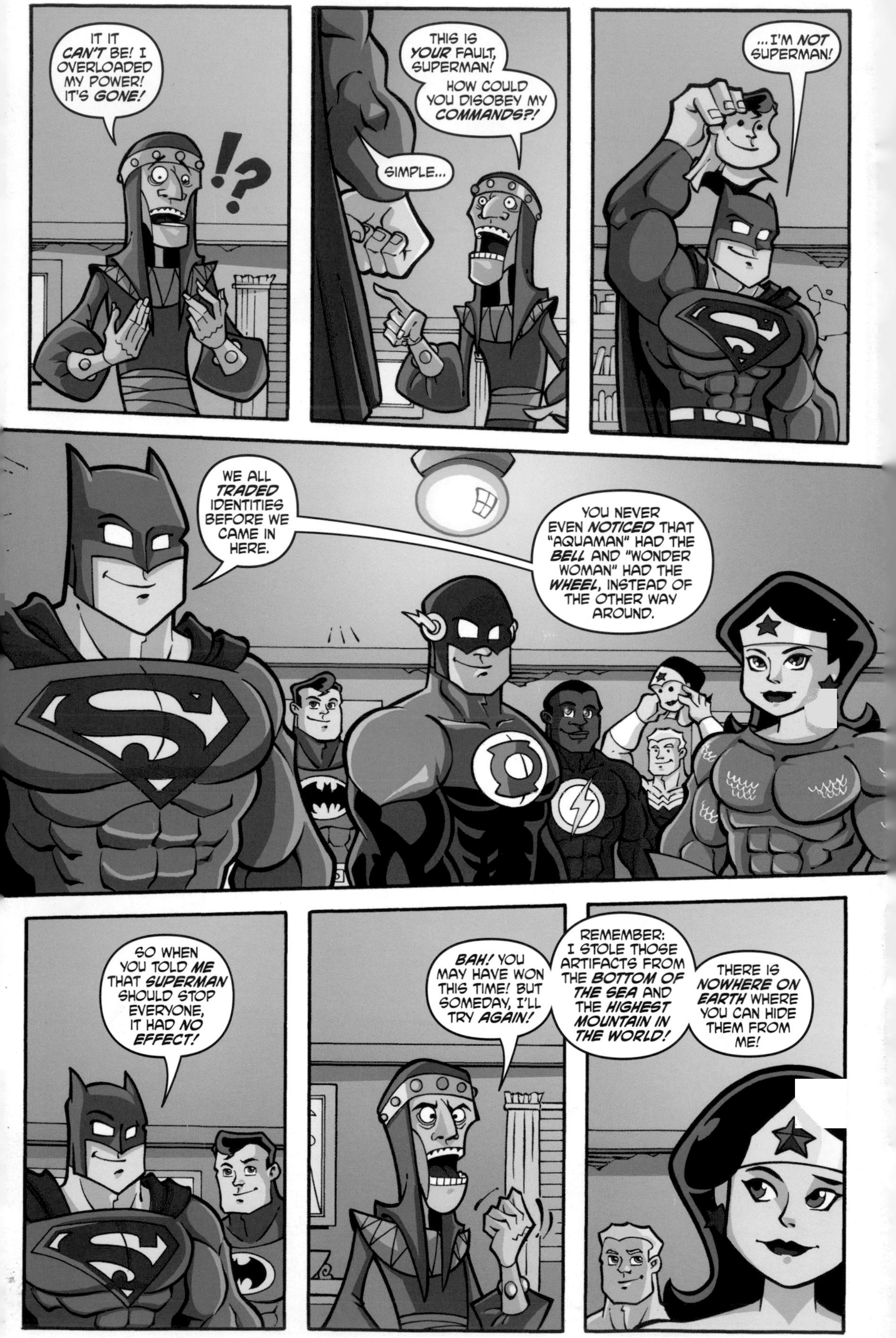
IT IT CAN'T BE! I OVERLOADED MY POWER! IT'S GONE!
!?
THIS IS YOUR FAULT, SUPERMAN!
HOW COULD YOU DISOBEY MY COMMANDS?!
SIMPLE...
...I'M NOT SUPERMAN!
WE ALL TRADED IDENTITIES BEFORE WE CAME IN HERE.
YOU NEVER EVEN NOTICED THAT "AQUAMAN" HAD THE BELL AND "WONDER WOMAN" HAD THE WHEEL, INSTEAD OF THE OTHER WAY AROUND.
SO WHEN YOU TOLD ME THAT SUPERMAN SHOULD STOP EVERYONE, IT HAD NO EFFECT!
BAH! YOU MAY HAVE WON THIS TIME! BUT SOMEDAY, I'LL TRY AGAIN!
REMEMBER: I STOLE THOSE ARTIFACTS FROM THE BOTTOM OF THE SEA AND THE HIGHEST MOUNTAIN IN THE WORLD!
THERE IS NOWHERE ON EARTH WHERE YOU CAN HIDE THEM FROM ME!

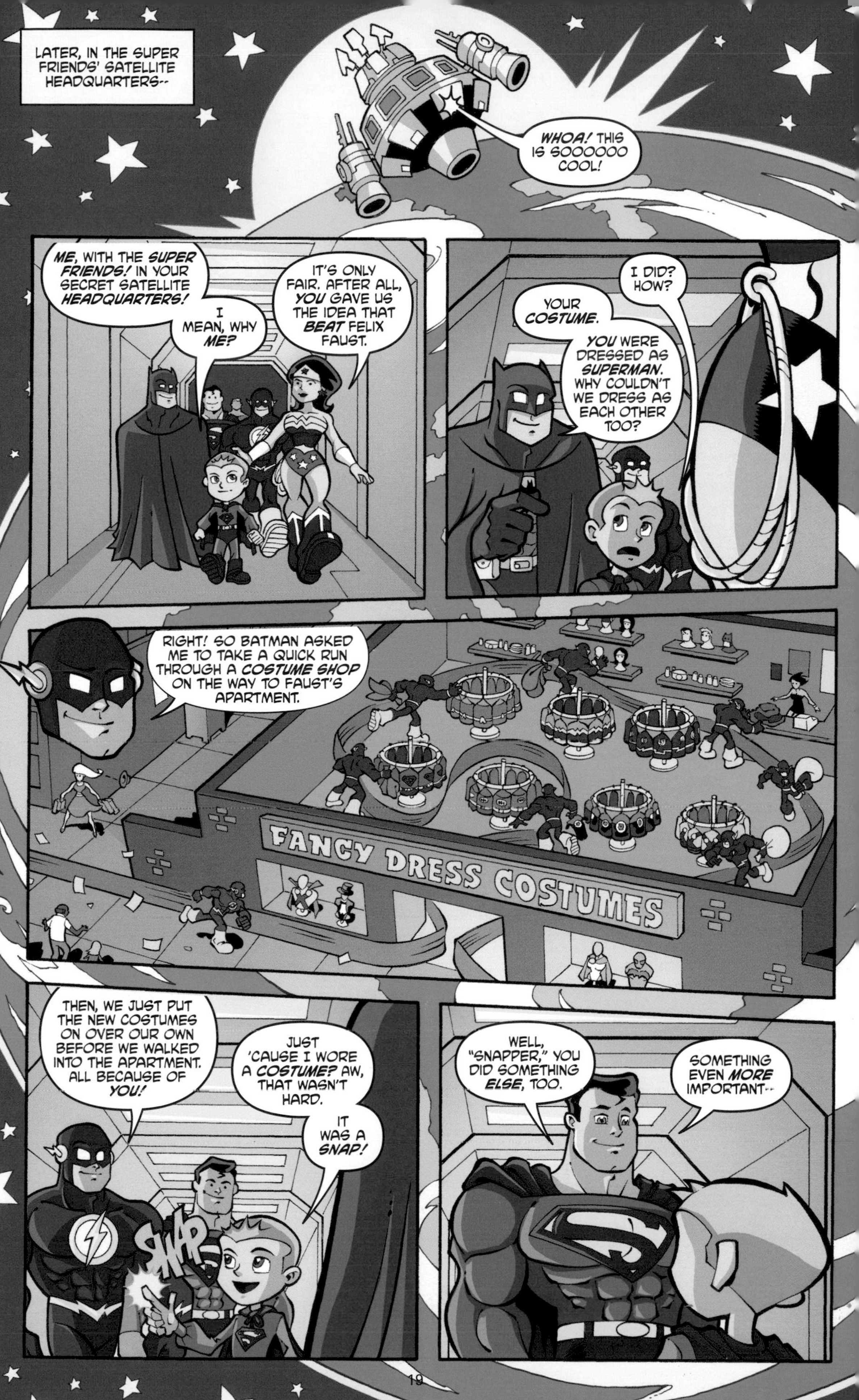
LATER, IN THE SUPER FRIENDS' SATELLITE HEADQUARTERS--
WHOA! THIS IS SOOOOOO COOL!
ME, WITH THE SUPER FRIENDS! IN YOUR SECRET SATELLITE HEADQUARTERS!
I MEAN, WHY ME?
IT'S ONLY FAIR. AFTER ALL, YOU GAVE US THE IDEA THAT BEAT FELIX FAUST.
YOUR COSTUME.
I DID? HOW?
YOU WERE DRESSED AS SUPERMAN. WHY COULDN'T WE DRESS AS EACH OTHER TOO?
RIGHT! SO BATMAN ASKED ME TO TAKE A QUICK RUN THROUGH A COSTUME SHOP ON THE WAY TO FAUST'S APARTMENT.
FANCY DRESS COSTUMES
THEN, WE JUST PUT THE NEW COSTUMES ON OVER OUR OWN BEFORE WE WALKED INTO THE APARTMENT. ALL BECAUSE OF YOU!
JUST 'CAUSE I WORE A COSTUME? AW, THAT WASN'T HARD.
IT WAS A SNAP!
SNAP
WELL, "SNAPPER," YOU DID SOMETHING ELSE, TOO.
SOMETHING EVEN MORE IMPORTANT--

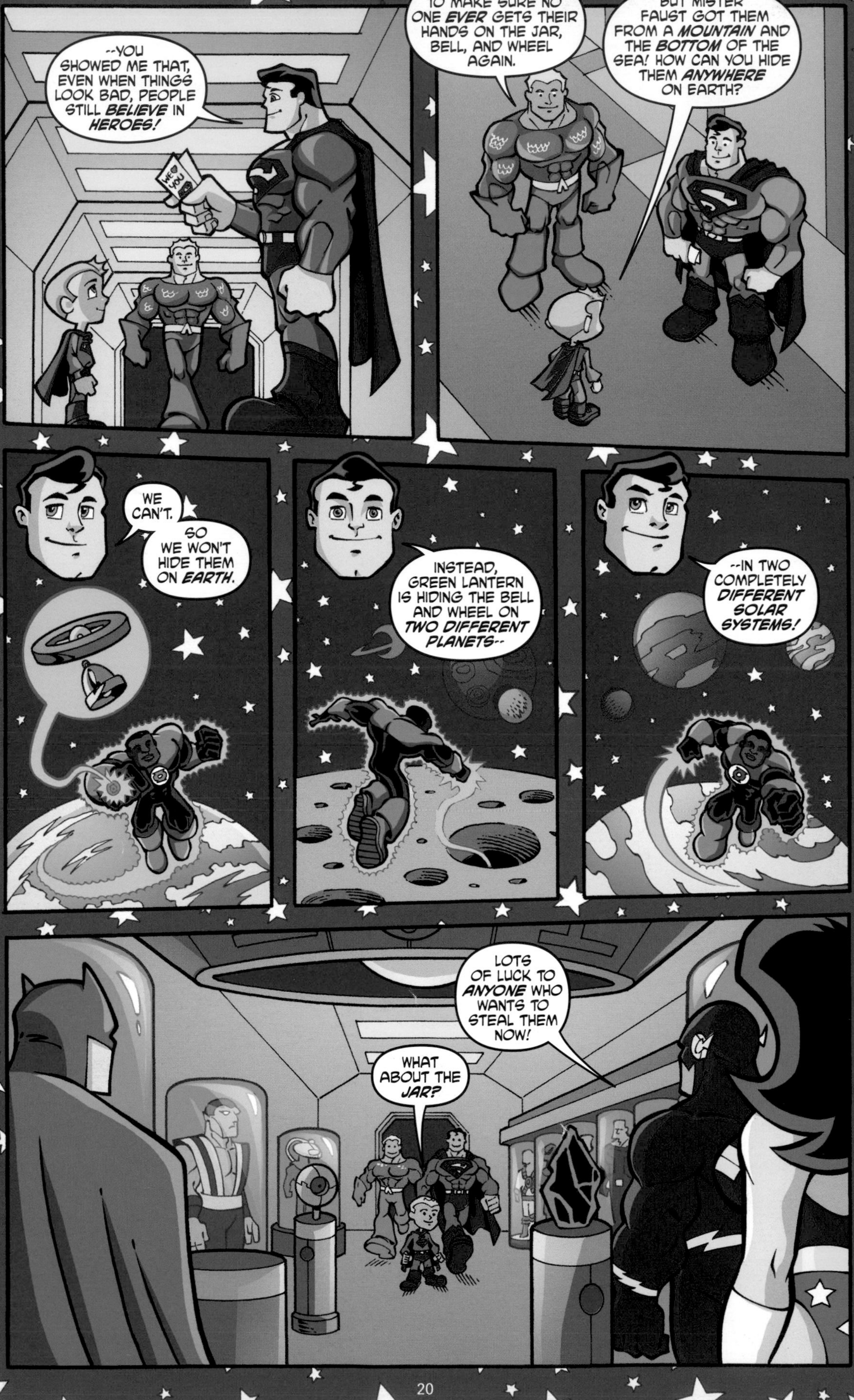
--YOU SHOWED ME THAT, EVEN WHEN THINGS LOOK BAD, PEOPLE STILL BELIEVE IN HEROES!
WE ♥ YOU
NOW, WE HAVE TO MAKE SURE NO ONE EVER GETS THEIR HANDS ON THE JAR, BELL, AND WHEEL AGAIN.
BUT MISTER FAUST GOT THEM FROM A MOUNTAIN AND THE BOTTOM OF THE SEA! HOW CAN YOU HIDE THEM ANYWHERE ON EARTH?
WE CAN'T.
SO WE WON'T HIDE THEM ON EARTH.
INSTEAD, GREEN LANTERN IS HIDING THE BELL AND WHEEL ON TWO DIFFERENT PLANETS--
--IN TWO COMPLETELY DIFFERENT SOLAR SYSTEMS!
LOTS OF LUCK TO ANYONE WHO WANTS TO STEAL THEM NOW!
WHAT ABOUT THE JAR?

WE DECIDED THE *JAR* WOULD BE SAFEST WHERE WE CAN KEEP AN *EYE* ON IT--

*--RIGHT HERE* IN OUR TROPHY ROOM!

SOUNDS LIKE YOU GOT IT ALL WRAPPED U-UUUUUUP!

EXCEPT *ONE* THING. I BELIEVE YOU MISSED A *ROLLER COASTER* BECAUSE OF ME.

SO *FIRST,* I OWE YOU A *RIDE!* AND THEN, IT'S BACK TO *WORK!*

AFTER ALL, THE *SUPER FRIENDS* STILL NEED TO GIVE PEOPLE SOMETHING TO *BELIEVE* IN!

# ATTENTION, ALL SUPER FRIENDS!

HERE'S THIS BOOK'S SECRET MESSAGE:

**PEVOY CYSOXRP ZBBU BEI CBY BINOYP**

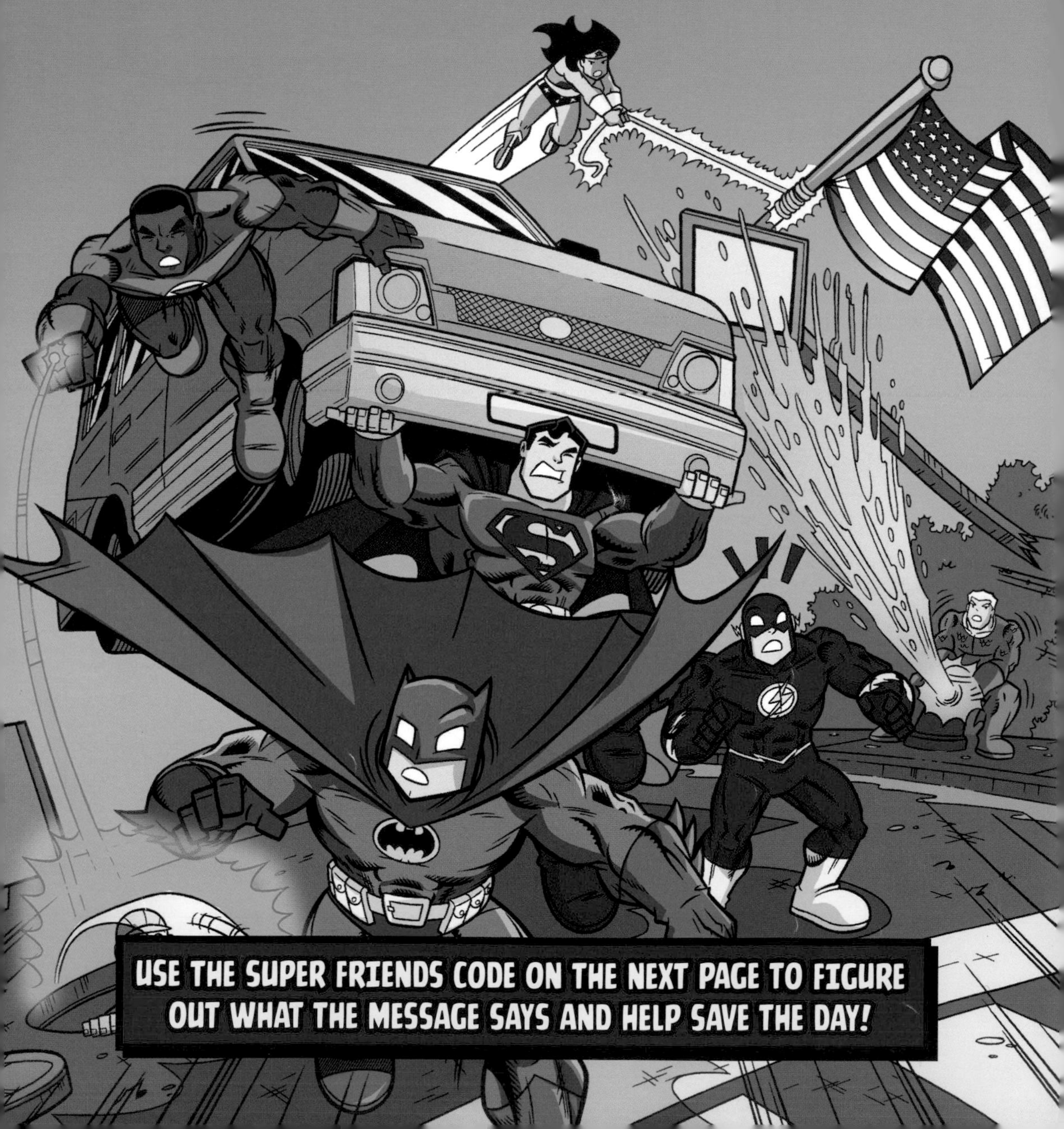

USE THE SUPER FRIENDS CODE ON THE NEXT PAGE TO FIGURE OUT WHAT THE MESSAGE SAYS AND HELP SAVE THE DAY!

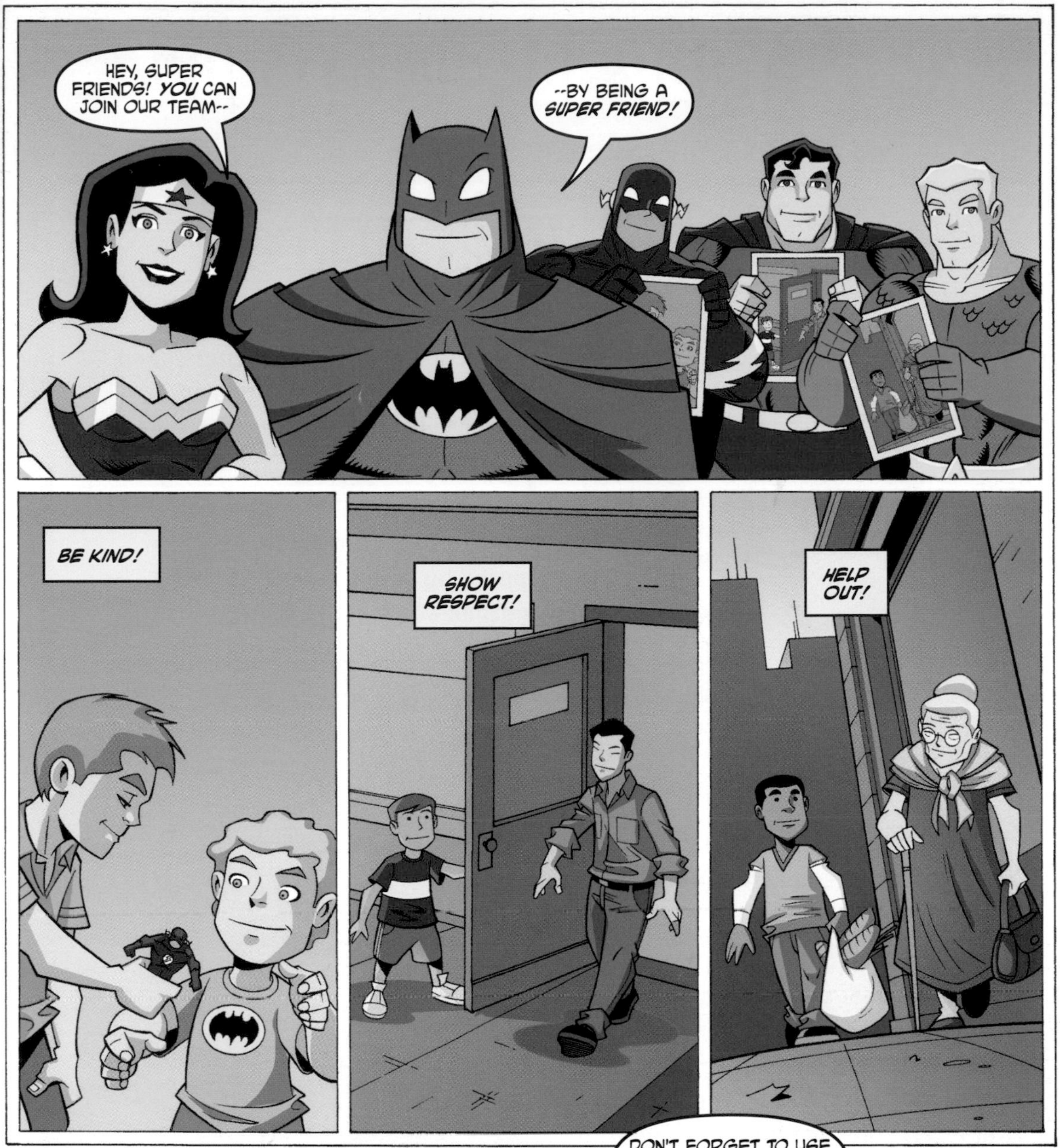
HEY, SUPER FRIENDS! YOU CAN JOIN OUR TEAM--
--BY BEING A SUPER FRIEND!
BE KIND!
SHOW RESPECT!
HELP OUT!

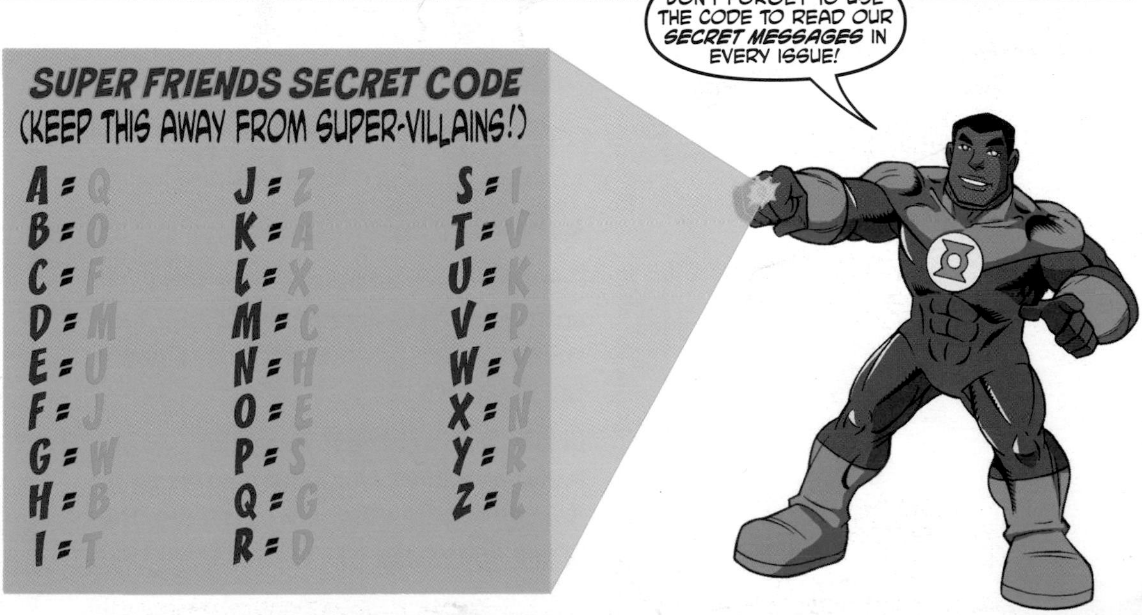
DON'T FORGET TO USE THE CODE TO READ OUR SECRET MESSAGES IN EVERY ISSUE!
SUPER FRIENDS SECRET CODE
(KEEP THIS AWAY FROM SUPER-VILLAINS!)
A = Q
B = O
C = F
D = M
E = U
F = J
G = W
H = B
I = T
J = Z
K = A
L = X
M = C
N = H
O = E
P = S
Q = G
R = D
S = I
T = V
U = K
V = P
W = Y
X = N
Y = R
Z = L

# KNOW YOUR SUPER FRIENDS!

## SUPERMAN

**Real Name:** Clark Kent

**Powers:** Super-strength, super-speed, flight, super-senses, heat vision, invulnerability, super-breath

**Origin:** Just before the planet Krypton exploded, baby Kal-EL escaped in a rocket to Earth. On Earth, he was adopted by a kind couple named Jonathan and Martha Kent.

## BATMAN

**Secret Identity:** Bruce Wayne

**Abilities:** World's greatest detective, acrobat, escape artist

**Origin:** Orphaned at a young age, young millionaire Bruce Wayne promised to keep all people safe from crime. After training for many years, he put on costume that would scare criminals - the costume of Batman.

## WONDER WOMAN

**Secret Identity:** Princess Diana

**Powers:** Super-strong, faster than normal humans, uses her bracelets as shields and magic lasso to make people tell the truth

**Origin:** Diana is the Princess of Paradise Island, the hidden home of the Amazons. When Diana was a baby, the Greek gods gave her special powers.

# GREEN LANTERN

**Secret Identity:** John Stewart

**Powers:** Through the strength of willpower, Green Lantern's power ring can create anything he imagines

**Origin:** Led by the Guardians of the Universe, the Green Lantern Corps is an outer-space police force that keeps the whole universe safe. The Guardians chose John to protect Earth as our planet's Green Lantern.

# THE FLASH

**Secret Identity:** Wally West

**Powers:** Flash uses his super-speed in many ways: he can run across water or up the side of a building, spin around to make a tornado, or vibrate his body to walk right through a wall

**Origin:** As a boy, Wally West became the super-fast Kid Flash when lightning hit a rack of chemicals that spilled on him. Today, he helps others as the Flash.

# AQUAMAN

**Real Name:** King Orin or Arthur Curry

**Powers:** Breathes underwater, communicates with fish, swims at high speed, stronger than normal humans

**Origin:** Orin's father was a lighthouse keeper and his mother was a mermaid from the undersea land of Atlantis. As Orin grew up, he learned that he could live on land and underwater. He decided to use his powers to keep the seven seas safe as Aquaman.

# CREATORS

## SHOLLY FISCH WRITER

Bitten by a radioactive typewriter, Sholly Fisch has spent the wee hours writing books, comics, TV scripts, and online material for more than 25 years. His comic book credits include more than 200 stories and features about characters such as Batman, Superman, Bugs Bunny, Daffy Duck, and Ben 10. Currently, he writes stories for Action Comics every month, plus stories for Looney Tunes and Scooby-Doo. By day, Sholly is a mild-mannered developmental psychologist who helps to create educational TV shows, web sites, and other media for kids.

## STEWART McKENNY ARTIST

Stewart McKenny is a comic artist living and working in Australia. He has worked on dozens of projects for the world's top comic book publishers, including Dark Horse, Marvel, and DC Comics. His credits include DC Super Friends, Star Wars: Clone Wars Adventures, and Captain America.

## PHIL MOY INKER

Phil Moy is a professional comic book and children's book illustrator. He is best known for his work on DC Comics, including Batman: The Brave and the Bold, DC Super Friends, Legion of Super-Heroes in the 31st Century, The Powerpuff Girls, and many more series.

## J. BONE COVER ARTIST

J.Bone is a Toronto based illustrator and comic book artist. Besides DC Super Friends, he has worked on comic books such as Spiderman: Tangled Web, Mr. Gum, Gotham Girls, and Madman Adventures. He is also the co-creator of the Alison Dare comic book series.

THEN MAYBE MY *POWER RI* CAN *SLOW HI* DOWN!

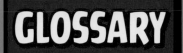

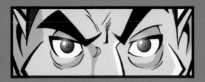

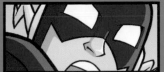

# GLOSSARY

*ancient* [AYN·shunt]-belonging to a time long ago

*artifacts* [ART·uh·fakts]-objects made or changed by human beings, especially a tool or weapon used in the past

*construction* [kuhn·STRUHKT·shuhn]-to build or make something

*criminal* [KRIM·uh·nuhl]-someone who commits a crime

*depths* [DEPTHS]-deepness, or a measurement of deepness

*identities* [eye·DEN·ti·tees]-who people are

*invisible* [in·VIZ·uh·buhl]-cannot be seen

*kryptonite* [KRIP·toe·nite]-any surviving fragment of the exploded planet Krypton, home of Superman

*marina* [muh·REE·nuh]-a small harbor where boats, yachts, etc., are kept

*mystic* [MISS·tik]-of or relating to magic

*refreshments* [ri·FRESH·muhnts]-drink and food

*satellite* [SAT·uh·lite]-a spacecraft that is sent into orbit around the Earth, the moon, or another heavenly body

*traffic* [TRAF·ik]-moving vehicles

*villains* [VIL·uhns]-wicked people, often evil characters in a story

*wizard* [WIZ·urd]-a person, especially a man, believed to have magic powers

I AM PR
TO USE ALL
FRIENDS' ABI
WOMAN'S
BATMAN

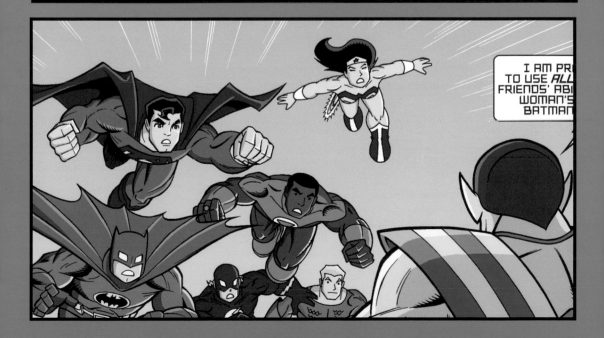

# VISUAL QUESTIONS & PROMPTS

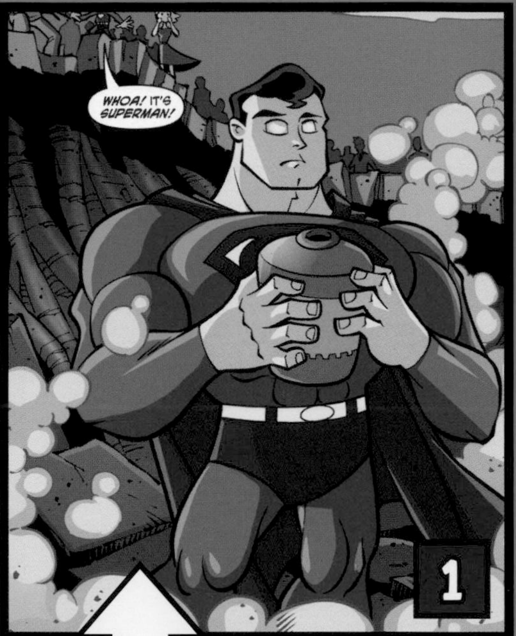
WHOA! IT'S SUPERMAN!
1

**1.** Sound words can add details and emotions to comics. What sound words could you add to the panel above? Make a list of at least three.

**2.** What visual clue shows that Wonder Woman is being controlled by Felix Faust in the panel below? Explain.

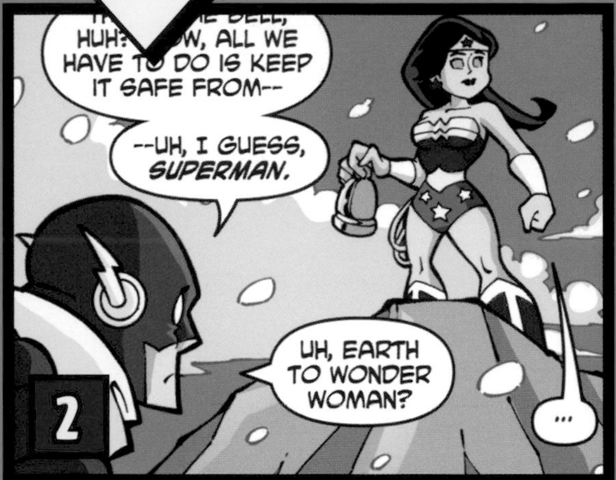
HUH? ALL WE HAVE TO DO IS KEEP IT SAFE FROM--
--UH, I GUESS, SUPERMAN.
UH, EARTH TO WONDER WOMAN?
...
2

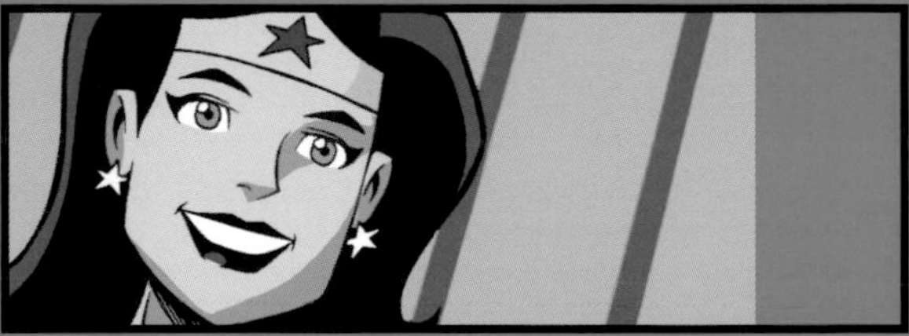

**3.** How are the Super Friends using their powers to help others? Which of these powers would you like to have most, and why?

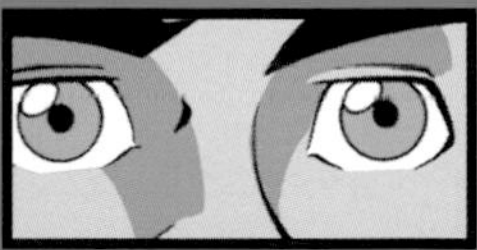

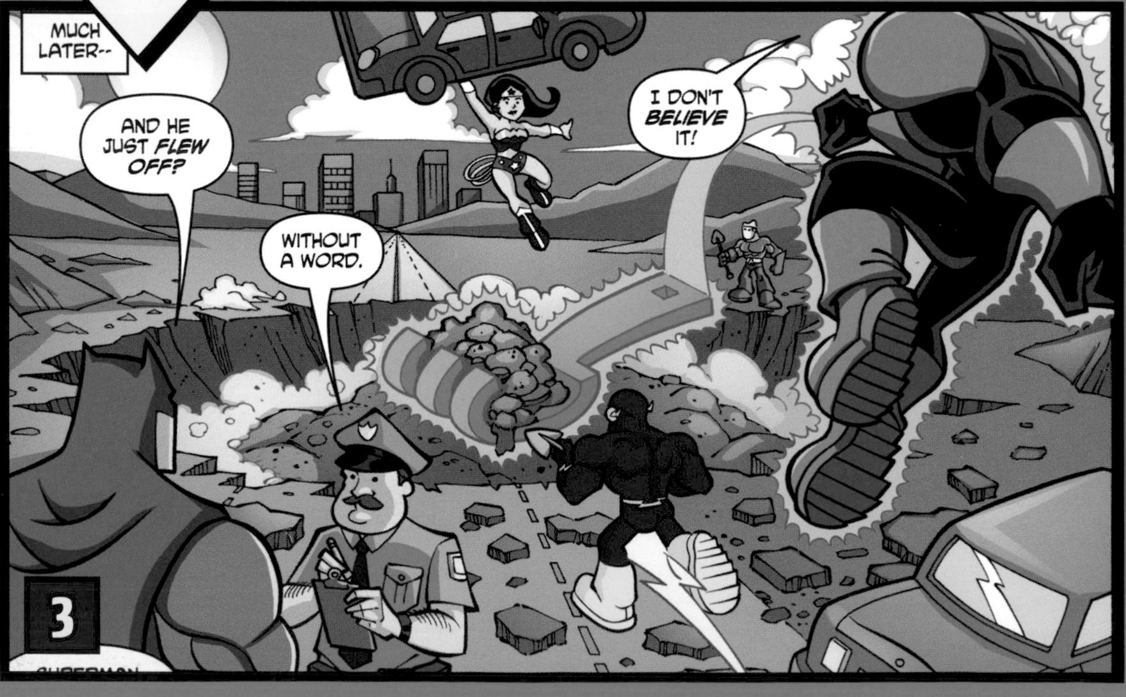
MUCH LATER--
AND HE JUST FLEW OFF?
WITHOUT A WORD.
I DON'T BELIEVE IT!
3

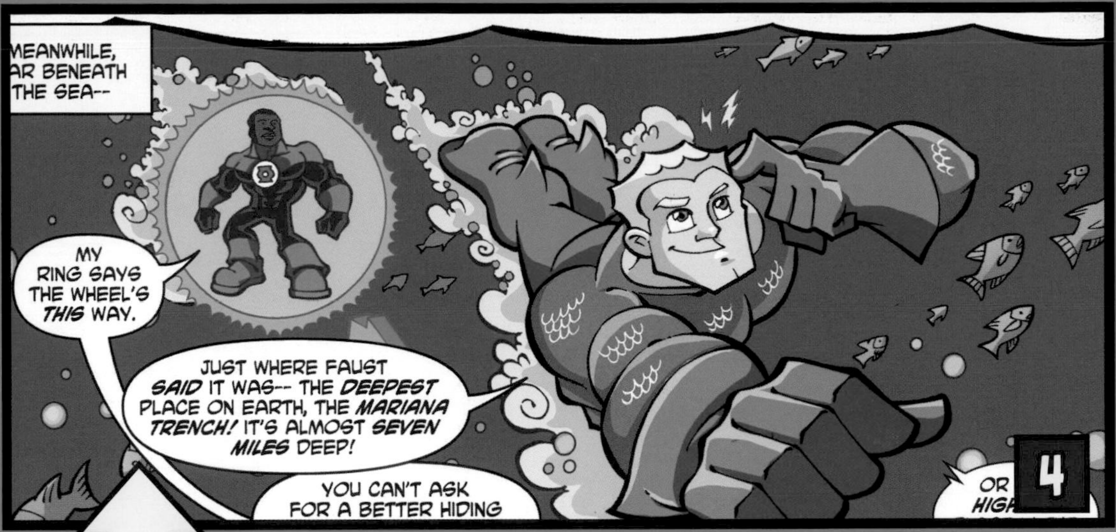
MEANWHILE,
AR BENEATH
THE SEA--
MY RING SAYS THE WHEEL'S *THIS* WAY.
JUST WHERE FAUST *SAID* IT WAS-- THE *DEEPEST* PLACE ON EARTH, THE *MARIANA TRENCH!* IT'S ALMOST *SEVEN MILES* DEEP!
YOU CAN'T ASK FOR A BETTER HIDING
OR
4

**4. What details are used in this panel, and others in the book, to show that the characters are underwater?**

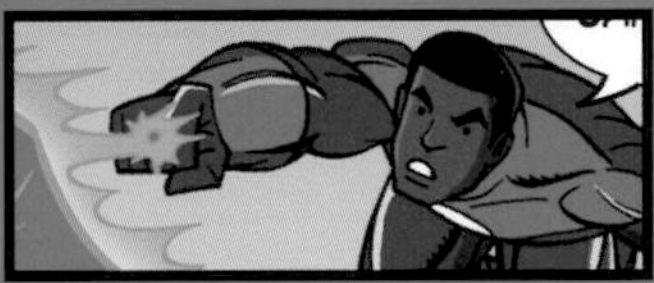

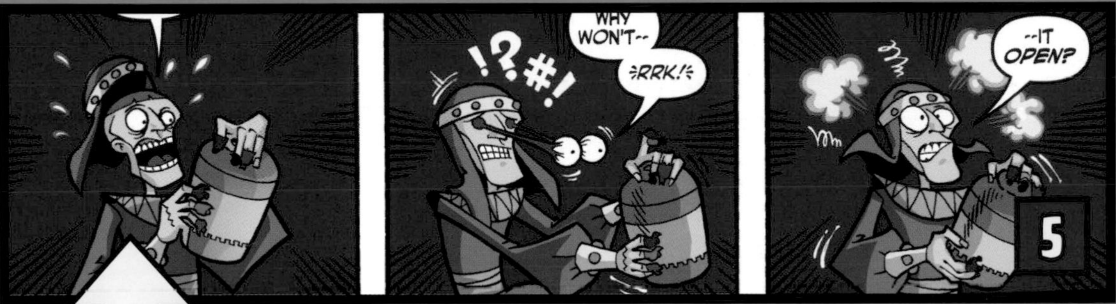
!?#!
WHY WON'T--
RRK!
--IT *OPEN?*
5

**5. Describe how Felix Faust feels in this series of panels. How do you know? What details show these emotions?**

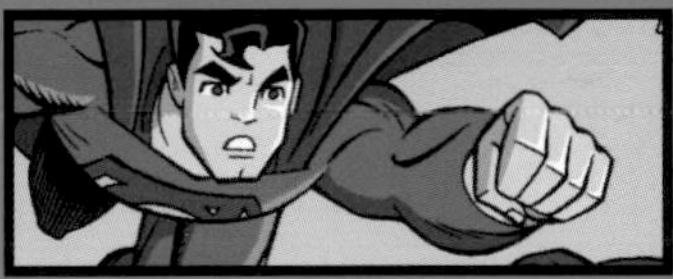

**6. In comics, the way a person looks and their expressions can sometimes tell the reader whether they are good or evil. Compare Wonder Woman to Felix Faust. How do their features differ? What does that information tell you?**

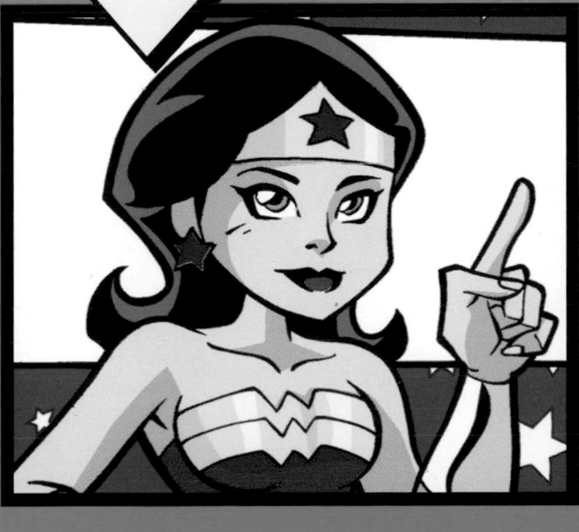

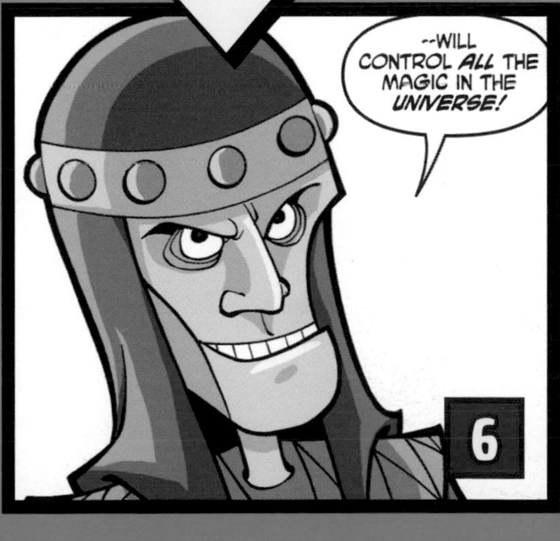
--WILL CONTROL *ALL* THE MAGIC IN THE *UNIVERSE!*
6

# READ THEM ALL!

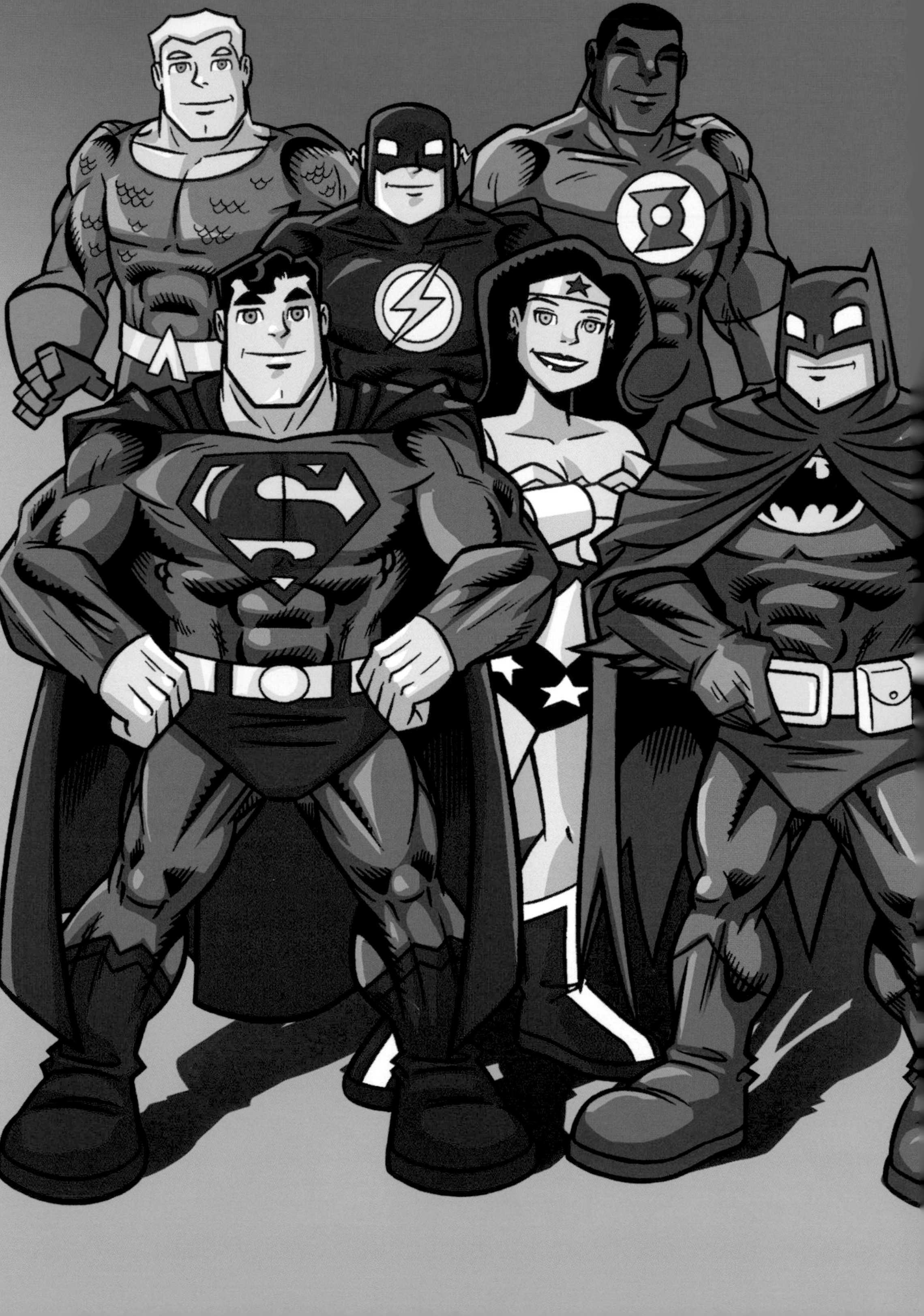

# DC SUPER FRIENDS™

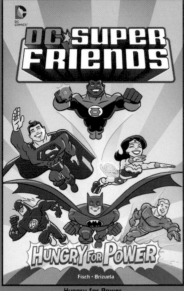

DC COMICS
DC SUPER FRIENDS
HUNGRY FOR POWER
Fisch • Brizuela

Hungry for Power

DC COMICS
DC SUPER FRIENDS
DINOSAUR ROUND-UP
Fisch • Ottolini • Staton

Dinosaur Round-up

DC COMICS
DC SUPER FRIENDS
WANTED: THE SUPER FRIENDS
Fisch • McKenny • Moy

Wanted: The Super Friends

DC COMICS
DC SUPER FRIENDS
APRIL FOOLS
Fisch • Brizuela

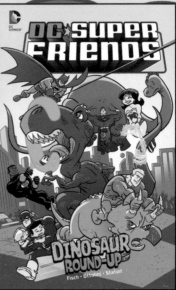

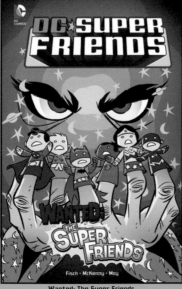

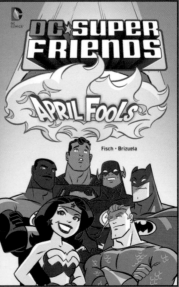

April Fools